The story of Anna Drei

Milena Milani

THE STORY OF ANNA DREI

translated from the Italian by
Graham Snell

Hutchinson of London

HUTCHINSON & CO (*Publishers*) LTD
178–202 Great Portland Street, London W1

London Melbourne Sydney
Auckland Johannesburg
Cape Town

*First published in Great Britain simultaneously by
Hutchinson & Co. and Arrow Books Ltd, 1970*

*This book has been set in Old Style, printed in Great Britain
on Antique Wove paper by Anchor Press, and
bound by Wm. Brendon, both of Tiptree, Essex*

ISBN 0 09 103620 8

For Thomas

I

One afternoon in that cold winter I stopped outside the Barberini cinema and opened my bag to see how much money I had and if it was enough to get in. A girl came up to me.

'If you're going in, I'll come too,' she said. 'I'm on my own.'

She introduced herself. 'I'm Anna Drei.'

I looked at her, I liked her, so we went in. It was dark inside: we groped our way to one of the back rows downstairs. It was a lousy film, the photography was poor, the dubbing ghastly.

'You see how they throw money away,' Anna Drei said. 'It's disgusting.' I agreed; I felt the same way as she did.

It was late when we came out. We went into a *rosticceria* in the piazza and had some pasta and a meat course; Anna Drei had a baked apple as well.

I kept throwing quick looks at her but without

taking in very much—the way you do with someone you've known a long time. I wasn't thinking about her either, I wasn't trying to find out about her, I just ate and then ate again, or else I drank a little water out of my glass. And Anna Drei was sitting there quietly too; her fresh face was relaxed, her hair was loose under her beret, her coat collar was turned up; she had dark eyes and pretty hands with slender fingers.

I walked with her to her *pensione* in the Piazza Mignanelli, up to the top floor; it was an odd place with big roof gardens. We met a young chap on the stairs.

'*Ciao*, Anna,' he said.

'*Ciao*,' she said.

She didn't tell me who the chap was, and I didn't ask. We went into her room: it was freezing; a divan, a handbasin, piles of books, newspapers, clothes, everything in a mess. Anna Drei sprawled on the bed. We lit cigarettes and drank a little *grappa*. I started coughing.

'Don't you like it?' said Anna Drei.

'It's a bit strong,' I said.

I was looking at the ceiling: it was cracked, it had once been pink but now it was faded.

Anna spoke up. 'Have you got time,' she said, 'a couple of minutes?'

'I've got plenty of time,' I said, 'as long as I like.'

'Good,' she said, 'well look here.'

She picked a packet up off the floor and opened

8

it: inside were some sheets of manuscript. The handwriting was irregular, spiky.

'Handwritten?' I said. 'That's unusual—most things are typed.'

'I know that all right, but who's got the money for typing?'

'You can hire a typewriter.'

'I don't like other people's things.'

I picked up a sheet of paper and looked at it.

'Is this your own stuff?' I said.

'My own stuff,' she replied.

'Would you lend it to me to read?'

'If you want to—I don't see why not.'

'Well then, I'll take it with me. It's late.'

'You can sleep here if you feel like it.'

'All right,' I said, 'I'll stay. But I was worried about the *pensione*. Won't they say anything?'

'Oh that doesn't matter,' she said, laughing. 'After all, you're not a man.'

Then she started undressing: she was lovely, well made and firm. She lent me a nightdress.

'It's hellishly cold,' she said. 'Don't be long.'

I undressed quickly and got into bed; we pulled the covers up over our noses.

Anna Drei fell asleep almost immediately. I stared for a bit into the dark, but I couldn't see a thing.

II

When I woke up the next morning Anna Drei was making breakfast.

'Good morning,' she said, 'you had a lot of sleep to catch up on.' She laughed. 'Do you know what time it is? It's nearly midday.'

I sat in a daze on the bed. 'Oh, please don't bother about me,' I said. 'I'll be going now.'

'There's some water there,' she said, 'but it's icy cold. Some milk will do us good. A pity there's no bread, but there's some biscuits.'

She laid the little table; it was littered with papers and there was a minute tablecloth. We ate hungrily. Then Anna went straight over to the bed and lay down and started smoking.

'What are you doing today?' she said.

'I don't know,' I said. 'I've got nothing fixed.'

'I haven't either. We could go for a walk.'

'Sure. It doesn't look too cold outside.'

'Rome's an extraordinary city,' said Anna Drei

as she put on her stockings . . . one had a hole in it.

'I haven't got time to darn it now,' she said.

We went out; it was two o'clock and the streets were almost empty. We went for a long walk up to the Villa Borghese, then along a deserted Via Veneto. Anna Drei walked with her hands in her coat pockets, her chin thrust forward, and an odd look of determination on her face.

'Just now I'm not in love,' she said suddenly.

'I'm not either,' I said.

'I could be,' she said, as if to herself, 'but I've decided to do away with it.'

'Do away with what?'

'With my life, for Christ's sake,' said Anna Drei, stopping suddenly. She clutched my sleeve and said, 'Because you—you wouldn't be fed up with life, by any chance?'

I shook my head. 'No, I'm not fed up, I enjoy life.'

Anna Drei started laughing. 'How old are you?' she said. 'I'm twenty-five. But I could be fifty.'

I didn't answer, I just looked at her. The look on her face upset me: surely she was lying.

She guessed what I was thinking. 'I'm not lying,' she said, 'but if you don't believe me, I won't say any more. In any case,' she said in a tone that was suddenly different, 'you're too young, you can't understand me. I haven't got any girl friends—you could be one though.'

She looked around the street with its bare trees. She sighed and said, 'What a nice street this is.'

When we got to the Tritone Fountain we quickly said goodbye to each other.

'I'll see you tomorrow,' Anna Drei said. 'Come to my place and we'll have something to eat.'

I wandered very slowly back home, thinking. That same evening I phoned her.

'Good evening,' I said. 'Yes, it's me. I wanted to read your manuscript. Can I come and get it?'

'Sure—come round. I've got some friends here.'

'I don't feel like seeing anyone, so I won't stay.'

Anna Drei brought me the manuscript out into the hall. She was in her dressing gown, and she was wearing lipstick.

'It's useful,' she said, 'because then nobody tries to kiss me.' She laughed. 'See you then.'

I went back home, closed the door of my room, put on the light, and straight away began reading.

III

'Yes, I'm a woman who writes. I'm different from most other women, maybe unique. Nobody's going to convince me, Anna Drei, that I'm not an exceptional woman. It's no good people laughing when they begin reading these words, or for them to say, She's mad, that one, or at least she's got a very high opinion of herself. It's no good. I know what I want to say.

'I was born of poor people, it's true, but I could have been the daughter of a king, of a rich and powerful man—it wouldn't have made any difference. Inside me I had boundless visions, I longed to reach the heights . . . it was something tremendously big, like the space surrounding the earth. I wanted by my own powers to penetrate the mysteries of the earth, this closed circle. I'll try to describe how I was, what I've learnt about myself, mysterious creature, born and still living, before it's too late. Why I want to do this I don't

know, but somehow I don't want to pass unob-
served, and spend my days as so many do, just
contenting themselves with trivial things.

'I studied the sky, and felt it inside me.

'I loved the sun, the sea, and men of flesh and
blood.

'Sometimes I felt as I walked that joy flowed
from under my feet, gushed out of me like some
liquid: an incredible joy which is made up of
nothing, of gentle unimaginable softness. I
travelled to the world's cities, I walked the streets
where everybody goes, but I was alone, it was
always me, with my face, my eyes, my sense of
wonder, and everything was created for me.

'They spoke of centuries, of ancient peoples, of
civilisations that had flourished and then vanished,
and I didn't believe any of it—except that it was
mine, even the past. I was a very strange woman,
and I have said so in these pages, as I did when I
looked at myself in the mirror.

'It was an oval-shaped mirror, with a dark
silver frame, and it had seen other faces for sure.
I saw my face, the colour of clear pearl, and my
eyelashes, my mouth, the little mark under my
eye and all my skin which had known caresses and
had been emptied of blood, purified. I looked at
myself—young, with loose dark hair, a strange
look of determination in my expression . . . the
urge to penetrate the impossible, where who
knows what God lives.

'How many times did I look at myself and I'd

have liked to slap and cuff myself, hurt myself and say, "Stop it, you're scaring me." There were nights when I groaned and nobody came, there was no sea, no mountains, not a sound to help me. Then I remembered the time when I was a little girl, my mother's kind face, and the faces of my elder brothers, who are scattered now all over the place—and a nostalgia for that magic time held my sobs back in my throat. My mother has gone now too, her words are lost, her gestures have disappeared, and her tenderness. Oh, how she used to say, "Anna, my Anna." When I was left alone I felt I was an aimless creature, with no purpose, uprooted from everything, ties and traditions, without a man, oh God, without a man who could speak to what I felt inside me, to my marvellous vision.

'Because I wasn't always like that: there was a time during my infancy when dreams filled my nights and in the darkness I saw future lives unfolding, lives that were miraculous and un-touched, and I was splendid and beautiful, dressed in gold like a statue.

'But it was too brief, too brief: on the bedroom walls there were enormous damp marks like live figures, phantoms dressed in silk, with here a face, there a piece of armour, and hunting animals, and trees loaded with fruit, and skies full of stars, and over everything a light grey colour, perhaps a desert of slate, like the roofs of houses, colourless.

'With all my secret thoughts on those obscure

15

phantoms, I grew up day by day, cut off from tradition, drifting into a sad calm where there was no future. Even then, in those early days when I first sensed the whys and wherefores of human life, even then a strange disbelief crept into me, a sense that everything was useless, that even love, maybe, might be vain and empty.

'Don't let anybody say that I, Anna Drei, have made all this sound difficult, not before reading right to the end, and understanding. It's never easy to judge, it takes knowledge and awareness, perhaps will-power. Not that I'm saying people really do have those gifts—that would be ridiculous—but I can always pretend they do, just to be nice. Anyway, such things don't matter: if this is my story, or rather the interpretation of a story, listen to it, it might be useful to somebody. Only my readers will, like me, have wept and searched and then laughed at themselves.

'After that preamble I can really begin.'

IV

'There's a house in a city, any city in this world, which is always my true home.

'So often when I was lost and mortally sad I got up in the morning thinking that I could go back there; even if the door was closed I had the key on me and there was nobody there. It was a big damp house, with cold rooms without much light, where everything was beautiful. I see myself as a little girl just a few years old, sitting on a narrow balcony, with rag dolls beside me, and my brothers playing with a ball down in the courtyard. As always, my mother is sewing her black dresses and from time to time she sings quietly, in a weak voice. My father isn't there: he's gone off with another woman, young and blonde, who laughs all the time and seems happy. They live in another town and they don't bother about us.

'I can hear my mother's voice saying, "Come on, Anna, that's enough now." It's getting dark;

I have watched the sky lose its beautiful colour, the roofs in the distance have faded, the strip of sea has turned pale. I sleep in my mother's bed: it has an iron bedhead and brass knobs, with a quilt and a silk bedspread, and two big feather pillows that your head sinks into. My mother takes me in her arms, undresses me, makes me say my prayers, then kisses me on the forehead. I lie there alone with a little light burning, which will be switched off later on when I'm asleep.

'And then I begin thinking about the fairylands which exist somewhere in the world and where the forests are dark blue and flowers grow all the year round. Wispy clouds float across the horizon, and rolling hills dotted with light-coloured shrubs surround the villages and the people who live in them are content with very little, as their heads are full of the sweetest dreams that are like coloured butterflies.

'I remember that old bedroom where I used to sleep, and which is still almost unchanged. There was a dusty cloth elephant, with a canopy on its back, and inside the canopy a tiny little queen with a gold crown, a sceptre and long tresses down her back. Often the little girl Anna would talk to the noble lady on the elephant and there would be strange conversations, especially at night.

'Anna: "Tell me, Queen, is the world big?"

'Queen: "The world is a nutshell. Only in the sky can you have distance and breathing space.

18

From my canopy with its drawn-up curtains I can see the sky: it is inside me, in my little papier mâché soul. When it gets dark and you go to sleep, and I'm left alone and the windows are closed, a strange glow lights up everything. And all things speak and wonder why they exist."

'Anna: "Tell me, Queen, by what mysterious destiny shall I grow up to question myself and struggle in vain against the law that governs us all?"

'Queen: "To grow up is to get smaller. And to accept is to understand the truth. In the mountains of the world there live beings that have dreamed dreams of power and become pure by looking within themselves as if into mirrors."

'Anna: "How incredible your pale voice sounds in the night, and I am thirsty for fables. So tell me how you came to be born on the cloth elephant, and who put you on Mummy's chest of drawers?"

'Then the Queen used to tell me her long story. There were cavaliers who came to fight and gathered flowers, and young women waiting; and in the distance were castles, and further away still cities . . . and there beside me the white hands of my mother mending a toy, with her usual care.

'Those were the hands that woke me, the hands that held me close, the hands that later on I folded in the shape of a cross in a coffin of pale-coloured wood. When mothers die, their children shrivel up; when our mothers leave us we are left

19

facing bare walls, and we feel like bashing our heads against them. I pictured my dead mother all dressed in black, with a gentle worn-out face that seemed just to have fallen asleep, and all around life went on: the sun beat on the window and the plants and flowers called the insects to give up their pollen.

'I wasn't there then: Anna Drei was already roaming the world, crying at night in frozen rooms that weren't like the one she had known as a little girl.'

V

'It's difficult to remember the city.

'To describe the sense of flickering danger that came to me from its smooth streets, its high deserted buildings, its shops with their big windows, and the painful spectacle of the sea held in by sea walls, always champing to burst through: I could do it all if I had the strength.

'But I see men: they pass by, they turn, they walk, a wheel that never stops revolving, that is the same at every latitude, and I, Anna Drei, stay here alone writing a story that gives me such pain and such enormous melancholy. There's no window in this place where I've chanced to camp with my exercise books and these books and my poor Queen on the elephant. It's a little temporary place, with four walls that shut me away at certain hours of the day and night from all the others who are curious about me. In here I think back to the distant city, how it looked to me when my mother took me out for my first walks and I was so young that you could count my years on the fingers of one hand.

'The street ran uphill, and at the top my heart was beating fast. There was an open space there with ancient benches where the old people from a nearby home used to sit; and behind the walls were gardens and orchards. From up there you could see the sea stretching vast beyond the port, and if the sun was beating down, the whole sea would swell and sparkle and glitter, and the dolphins would go mad and boats with white sails race over the water.

'With my mother I was relaxed. But alone I had fears and disappointments that came and went all the time because I had an instinctive need to know, and I wanted to grow up immediately, to be of an age and have experience so that I could even cross the sea and see if there was land on the other side.

'But what land did I find later on?

'New countries attracted me, but what dread crept into my heart.

'In desperation I searched, and the more I searched the less there was left for me, and nowhere in the world did I find anything that could bring me peace.

'The city was so beautiful—*that city*; there's no point in my describing it, saying what it's called, naming its streets and mountains, and placing it in some precise documented part of the world.

22

They will say, "Fantasy." And I will reply, "Fantasy."

'In any case, everything is known about us—and about me too, everything can be found out—that my name is Anna Drei, where I was born and when, who were my parents, who are my brothers and sisters, if I've been ill, if I had or still have money, if I have known any men, if I've belonged to them. Oh, everything is clear, nothing can be hidden, we are labelled worse than prisoners, we all carry numbers on our backs. I'd like to tear myself away from this maddening monotony, I'd like to find the roads of the sky, tracks to follow like those in the desert, with sand and more sand and fairy visions. Perhaps old untamed instincts are boiling up in me again. I tried to suppress them, to be like everybody else, a nothing in the great game of existence. I was masked then, and nobody realised it, and behind the holes of my eyes my real face was suffering, and I had nothing to save me, no hope, nothing.

'But the city, the city that I knew as a little girl, and all the people there were still alive—they seemed good, they left me free to think.

'My mother used to say, "Thank God for giving you life. God lives up in the sky."

'Anna would reply, "The birds fly fast in the sky and the trees move their branches. The scent of flowers floats across the sky."

' "Anna, my Anna," my mother would say, "the

23

goodness in people's hearts is a gift from God. I'll ask Him if you can have it."

'Anna would reply, "By being good we only harm ourselves; it shuts us in and leaves us no way out. I breathe the air, the air makes me grow, my body gets taller, and I acquire more knowledge." '

VI

I put the manuscript back in the packet. It was late, but I didn't feel at all like sleeping. I had a great urge to see Anna again. By now it was dark, and the lamp threw a harsh area of light in the room; the light was almost white, unreal. I thought that maybe Mario wouldn't come home; after all, I had slept the previous night at Anna's place, and if Mario had come home and found I wasn't there, he must have been very angry.

Then Mario came in—he didn't make too much noise. He said, '*Ciao.*'

'*Ciao,*' I replied. He began undressing: he was wearing a blue shirt with thin white stripes.

'It's cold,' he said. 'Move over.'

I made room for him by pressing up against the wall. Mario's feet were frozen. We lay there without moving, me with arms by my sides, and Mario with his hands behind his head. I was

25

looking at the window in front of me, with the curtains drawn—they were yellowish and rather dirty.

'We must have them cleaned,' I said.

Mario started laughing. He laughed suddenly, with no warning, hysterically. Then he slapped me, and slapped me again before I could do anything. I had my legs flexed against him, trying to push away, but he kept hitting me. My face was burning, and my head ached. Then I started crying, but not very much and not so that he could hear.

We were exhausted when we fell asleep. Mario hadn't said a thing, he hadn't asked me any questions, yet I knew he was very angry with me.

I woke up after what seemed a long, long sleep, but in fact it had only been a few hours. I could feel Mario's body beside me: it was warm, and he was breathing heavily. No particular thoughts crossed my mind, except for a vague recollection of Anna, and how well we had slept together, she and I, and what Anna was writing, extraordinary creature. I could sense that winter had come too, and the streets of Rome were windy, and the cold froze your brain and ringed it with ice.

I loved those streets when I went out alone in the early spring or in the autumn, and there was a tepid sun, and the leaves on the trees were all green, boys and girls were out in their Sunday clothes, and high above everything was that beautiful blue sky. Now the sky was cloudy, like stone all over, and people were hurrying past wearing horrid overcoats, and the trees were lifeless. I remembered certain days when I used to walk along by the Tiber and sit in quiet spots on the embankment where the golden water flowed lazily, and where high-spirited youths swarmed on the boats from the canoe clubs, and the houseboats were hung with flags, and people sat in deck-chairs enjoying the sunshine.

Rome stretched along the banks of its river with particular benevolence. It seemed a strong city, its buildings solid, the domes of its churches massive; it was built out of fierce eternal toil, as if its builders had thrown their whole lives into the task of creating it.

I don't know whether I realised it, but the city had been mine for only a short time; I still had to discover it, to pry behind its ruins, behind the high green walls of the Villa Celimontana, haven for lovers. I used to like going there with a group of young people, to keep quiet and listen to the birds singing up in the branches. Sometimes my companions used to imitate the birdsong.

Mario didn't like walking—he was lazy and often violent, and frequently he got all mystical or else sank into black thoughts about himself and perhaps about me. He was rich; he used to enjoy impressing me with his wealth. In spite of all that money, we lived in that poor room in the Piazza di Pietra; there was often money in the

27

drawers and on the table, but we never touched it. I myself didn't bother about it, and sometimes, for a joke, I used to throw ten-thousand-lira notes out of the window. Some of them used to flutter down on to the roofs below.

VII

Anna Drei phoned while I was getting dressed to go over to her place.

'Did you read any of it?' she asked.

'The first few pages—not very much.'

'Good. Bring it over, will you—I need it.'

So I went out with the manuscript under my arm. At Anna's place, I put it on top of some books.

'I'm sorry I can't read the rest,' I said, 'but if you need it . . .'

'You can read it some other time,' she said. 'I realise now I wrote some stupid things.'

We had something to eat. After a bit Anna Drei said, 'Do you sleep with a man over at your place?'

I said I did, that there was a man, and his name was Mario.

'What sort of a man is he?' asked Anna Drei.

I didn't answer—I would have hated answering. I didn't know myself what sort of a man he was.

'The other day you said you weren't in love,' said Anna Drei.

'That's true, I'm not in love.'

'So why do you live with him?'

I didn't answer that question either, because I didn't know the answer.

'Come and stay here,' said Anna Drei. 'We could fix it up for the two of us.'

'Stay here all the time?' I said. 'But I'd get on your nerves.'

'Don't bother about me,' she said. 'In summer the roof gardens are a mass of flowers.'

VIII

So I told Mario I was moving in with Anna Drei. I told him the address too—Piazza Mignanelli 6, on the top floor.

Mario laughed; he was lying on the bed with his overcoat over him. 'Anna Drei,' he said, 'I expect she's some artist or other living in a garret, and you, you poor fool, go running after her.'

I was packing my things, throwing them any old how into a case. And yet I had had some lovely times with Mario, times when we didn't have a thought in our heads, when our hearts felt nothing any more and only our bodies seemed to count, times when we had that youthful delusion of happiness and our flesh glowed all over.

But in other ways Mario was a strange man and often I didn't understand him: his habit of smiling at the most unexpected moments almost scared me, and that look of his that used to wander I don't know where, and seemed to slip past me, ignoring me—that look of his used to irritate me.

We argued about futile things—like me not getting him a book when he wanted it, or hiding his cigarettes—and he used to break all the mirrors in my handbags. But at night we clung together; like two people drowning we used to say each other's names, our hands invented movements, our mouths words. But it couldn't last like that, I knew, and Mario knew it too.

I was packing my things and he wasn't saying anything: he was still lying lazily on the bed, although he was cold. Sometimes he looked at me. He had eyes that slanted towards his temples, rather big eyes of a light hazel colour, with long lashes . . . once I had trimmed them with scissors. 'They'll grow even longer,' I had told him, and in fact they did.

How odd—here was Mario, a man for me, but I was going away. With him I had eaten, slept, done all the things that women do with men, but now I was going away. And at times I had loved that room.

I looked round it once again: I saw the curtains, and I said they needed cleaning, and that I'd told him before, and he ought to remember. Mario said he hadn't forgotten, that I shouldn't worry about him. Then I opened the door and went downstairs.

My case wasn't heavy, but I felt as if I had a big stone inside me. It made my arms hurt.

IX

When I arrived, Anna Drei wasn't at home. At the street door to the *pensione* I met the young man I had seen a few days before—the one who had said *ciao* to Anna.

'Good afternoon,' he said, 'are you coming here too?'

'Yes, I'm coming too,' I said. 'I'm staying with Anna Drei.'

He came up with me and sat casually on the bed. He told me his name was Antonio and he was a student. He said he came from Terni, and he was twenty-two. He told me all about himself, in half an hour, while we were waiting for Anna.

His mother was in Terni—she was a widow—and he was the only son; there was a daughter of sixteen, who was a dressmaker.

'Terni's only a little town,' he said. 'It was badly damaged in the war. Our house is behind the piazza—we've got a little flat on the second floor. It wasn't touched.'

When he spoke there was a slight movement at the corner of his mouth, like a nervous tic. I was fascinated, and instead of listening to what he said I was waiting for the movement to start up again. He noticed I was watching: he said he'd had it since he was a little boy, and his schoolmates had teased him about it.

He told me, too, about university; he said you couldn't understand the lectures and the professors didn't bother overmuch. He wasn't a bad-looking boy, far from it—he was blondish, with curly hair in thick little waves; he was quite stocky with broad shoulders, and he had big red hands with very short nails. He was dressed in brown, and he was wearing a raincoat.

'My room's the one that looks on to the other roof garden, towards the kitchen,' he said, 'but we're very close. It's lucky finding lodgings so near the centre these days.'

Then he pulled out some photographs. One was of his mother—a small woman sitting on a low wall. 'I took it,' said Antonio, 'when we went for a drive in the country. It was such a nice day. My sister came too, with a couple of her girl friends.'

He showed me his sister with her two friends. 'That's her by the tree,' he said. 'The other two are Carla and Gina.'

'Gina—she's really beautiful,' I said. 'Is she blonde?'

'A natural blonde,' said Antonio, raising his voice slightly. 'Blonde—you should see it. A marvellous colour.'

'Who's this blonde we're talking about?' Anna Drei cut in sharply, as she suddenly appeared, loaded with parcels and nearly tipping them over Antonio.

'Out, out of here,' she almost shouted. Antonio went straight out, saying goodbye to me with a movement of his eyes.

'You've no idea how stupid that boy is,' said Anna Drei. 'What was he telling you?'

'He was talking about a girl friend of his sister's called Gina. He showed me a photograph of her.'

'He's always on about something,' said Anna. 'He can never stay in his own room. And he's a gossip—he knows everything that goes on in the *pensione*, and in other places too.'

'I must say he seemed a nice boy to me.'

Anna Drei gave a nervous shrug of her shoulders. 'A nice boy, a nice boy—what are you talking about? What's all this nonsense about nice boys?'

I didn't say anything. Anna Drei was upset about something, that was obvious.

X

After we'd had supper we went out.

It was a fantastically clear moonlight night. The whole city was white, white and cold, as if invisible snow had blotted out every footmark, every dark point, along the streets and on the buildings. There weren't many people about, and the occasional street lamps were very dim—or so they appeared in that strange half-light.

I had something weighing on my heart. So did Anna.

Mario came vividly back to my mind—and that odd laugh of his; and also other men I scarcely knew, like that boy Antonio I had talked to that afternoon, and another one I had known for years, an old school friend. Perhaps Anna had the same thoughts as me . . . she certainly had some odd ideas about love.

Suddenly she gripped my arm, in her usual way, forcing me to stop. I shot a look at her: I was frightened. How big and dark her eyes were in that white light!

'What's the matter, Anna?' I said. 'What's going on?'

She didn't say anything. I could sense there were words forming in her mind, and I felt I ought to help her so that the words would take shape on her lips.

'It's difficult,' she said at last, 'it's so difficult.'

'What's difficult?' I said. (Who is this other Anna? I was thinking.)

We walked on, up the Corso Umberto towards the Via del Mare; then all of a sudden we turned back.

'Why don't we go up by the Colosseum?' I said. 'It'll be marvellous in this moonlight.'

'All right, let's go,' said Anna. 'It's all the same to me.'

There were couples there who weren't feeling the cold. Some were sitting on stone blocks, others had gone into dark corners. Those arches and those great stone masses filled me with dread: I felt abandoned, as if I had got lost, so I talked to Anna, I told her some of my secrets, and she smiled quietly as she listened. But very soon she suggested we should go back.

I was telling her that once, out at sea, I had seen a dolphin. I don't really know why I talked about the sea—it seemed so far away on that winter night in Rome, like some far distant time, instead of only the previous summer.

'It was a little dolphin,' I said, 'because it didn't overturn the boat.'

'Who was in the boat?' Anna asked.

'I was.'

'You were on your own?' she insisted.

'No, of course I wasn't on my own,' I replied . . . and I was thinking that Mario had been there.

'That Mario was with you,' Anna said.

I said yes he was, and I told her everything about Mario.

'But you're in love,' said Anna, 'you do nothing but talk about him. Why do you talk about him so much?'

'I don't know why. I talk about him because we get on to that subject—that's all. But I'm not in love, not at all, and anyway I told you so the other day.'

'What was it like,' broke in Anna, 'what was it like that time in the boat?'

'I don't know, but I enjoyed it. He and I were happy in those days.'

'And afterwards,' asked Anna, 'what happened afterwards?'

'Nothing happened—nothing ever happened.'

It was strange, after all, talking about Mario, after leaving him so suddenly. It meant it wasn't so easy to forget him.

'Where did you live with this Mario?' said Anna.

'Piazza di Pietra, in a *pensione*.'

'He'll be there now. What sort of chap was he—

was he a creature of habit?'

'Oh, I wouldn't know, but he didn't keep regular hours.'

'I'd like to meet him . . . just casually, for my own reasons.'

'If you like we can go and see him now. It's not very far.'

So we went. The street door was open and as I was going in the porter's little boy waved to me through the window.

XI

Mario was still lying on the bed with his overcoat over him—as if he had never moved. As soon as he saw me, he said something about the curtains.

'I've sent them to be cleaned. I told Pina to see to it.' Pina was the woman who came in to do the room.

'Good,' I said. Then I said, 'This is Anna Drei.'

'Fine,' Mario said. 'Make yourself at home.'

Anna Drei sat on the end of the bed, and I sat near Mario. The chairs (there were three of them) were piled with stuff.

'So, Mario,' I said, 'what have you been doing since I went away?'

Mario raised his eyebrows. 'I haven't been doing anything at all.'

'We've been for a walk,' I said. 'Me and Anna. There's a moon tonight. It's cold, but it's not too bad.'

'It's nice walking along the streets,' said Anna

Drei. 'There aren't many people about either.'

'I've been here all the time,' said Mario.

'Aren't you cold?' I said.

'A bit,' replied Mario, 'but with the overcoat . . . besides, I've still got my clothes on.'

'Winter's over now,' said Anna Drei. 'Rome's lovely in the spring.'

'They say it's going to get cold again,' I said. 'The weather men said so.'

'They talk a load of rubbish,' Mario said.

He was looking vacantly round the room. So was Anna Drei.

Something was weighing on all three of us, and I didn't know what it was. With the curtains taken down, the window looked enormous. I found myself counting some little marks somebody had scratched with a pin on the whitish paintwork . . . I counted more than fifteen.

Then Mario looked at his watch. 'If you need to be going,' he said, turning back to us, 'don't stand on ceremony. I can't come with you.'

'Yes, let's go,' I said. '*Ciao*, Mario.'

'*Ciao*,' Mario said. 'Good night.'

'Good night,' said Anna Drei.

XII

All the way back we said nothing. Anna Drei seemed bored and rather depressed; she had dark rings around her eyes.

'I've got a headache,' she said suddenly. 'I'll take something for it when I get home.'

I was looking round . . . at the streets, the outlines of the buildings—and at some dark corners which gave me goose pimples. I didn't know why I was so frightened by the dark. The moon had risen: it was casting its light on other places. There was a great silence—no more cars passed, and no more people.

I kept thinking again and again of those little marks scratched on the window-frame. I wondered who had gone to so much trouble, and I was thinking, too, of what Mario hadn't said: perhaps he hadn't liked Anna Drei.

Anna Drei—what an absurd, complicated girl.

'Anna,' I said, 'will you give me your manuscript when we get home? I'd like to read some more of it.'

'All right,' she replied, 'tonight I'm going straight to bed—I've got a headache.'

We walked close together, but not touching; Anna was a little taller than me. I could smell the shampoo in her hair.

'You've washed your hair,' I said.

'Yes—yesterday, last night.'

'I must go and get mine done.'

'If you like you can wash it at home. I've got an electric dryer.'

'Good—I'll do it tomorrow morning.'

'That Mario,' Anna said, 'he's an odd sort of chap.'

We walked up the stairs of the *pensione*; there were several flights, so we stopped for a moment.

'You . . . and that Mario,' Anna said, 'you must be wondering why you ever moved in with him.'

'I don't know. But I've moved out now.'

(Mario was still on the bed, with his overcoat over him, and with the light burning, and he'd be thinking. But I didn't know what Mario could be thinking about.)

'I'm going to stay here now,' I said, going in with Anna Drei.

We switched on the light: the room seemed bright and cheerful.

'What a lovely smell of cooking,' I said. 'I'll open the window for a minute.'

Fresh air came in, five seconds of fresh air.

Then we closed the window because it was night-time and cold.

'When you get down to it,' Anna said, 'why are we born?'

'It's difficult to explain,' I replied. 'I wonder how many have tried.'

'I was born, and I've got a headache,' Anna said. 'I'll take something for it and try to sleep. If I sleep I don't think. If I don't think I'm happy. I like to be happy.'

'So do I.'

I sat down with Anna's manuscript. Anna went to bed.

'Don't read too much of it,' Anna said. 'I don't think it's worth it.'

'You never know,' I said.

I steadily turned the pages, reading slowly; from time to time I stopped and gazed into space. I caught sight of myself in a mirror. How small my face was, small and pointed. What a little woman I was.

I looked at Anna lying there in bed. Her body made a small hump under the blankets, and her hair lay spread out on the pillow. I had a tight feeling in my heart. Like so many people in the world, Anna would be dead one day. And I would be dead—yes, perhaps me too. Anna would stop breathing, her body would lie perfectly still under the bedclothes. How horrible.

I called her. 'Anna,' I said. 'Anna.'

She raised herself a little on one elbow.

'What's the matter?' she said. 'I was asleep.'

'Nothing's the matter—I was imagining you were dead.'

'I often do that myself, but I'm still alive.'

She started laughing, but then she said that laughing made her head ache.

'Oh, it hurts, it's terrible, that pill didn't do any good.'

'Sometimes it takes a while to work. But you must lie quiet.'

'I'll be quiet. I'd like to have a nice dream if I can.'

'I don't often have nice dreams,' I said, 'but sometimes I dream of butterflies.'

'Romantic dreams,' Anna said. 'I often dream of snakes.'

She told me about a snake that had tried to eat her. She climbed a tree and up there she could see the sea and a city.

'The roofs in that city were all red, but red like fire, and then I realised it was burning. I shouted for somebody to put the fire out, but nobody heard. In any case, there was nobody about.'

I told her about a dream of mine: I was in a field and it was Sunday, I was wearing a nice white dress and I had my hair long down my back. There was a little boy holding my hand, and the trees were all in flower. I told her we caught a butterfly that had golden wings. I told her a lot about that butterfly, but Anna went off to sleep, so I didn't say any more. I began reading what she had written. I read and I didn't understand very much, not because it was difficult, but maybe because other things kept coming into my mind— Mario, the streets in the moonlight, and what I was going to do the next day.

XIII

The next day I went on reading Anna Drei's manuscript.

I was on my own. Anna had gone out early—she said she would be back in the evening because she had lots of things to do. I didn't know what things, and she didn't explain. I stayed in all day and ate some fruit. Early in the afternoon Antonio came and knocked on the door to the roof garden. He came in and we chatted a bit.

He had a letter, which he showed me: it was from Gina, his sister's friend.

'They went out into the country to buy some eggs,' Antonio said. 'And they're going to send me some here in Rome. I'll give you some when they turn up.'

I thanked him. I said I was very fond of fresh eggs.

Antonio talked about a couple of friends of his who came to his place to study; one was called

Gianni—he was the son of an engineer—and the other was called Stefano.

'Gianni's an odd sort of guy. If he comes today I'll introduce you. He doesn't say much, but he's very intelligent. So is Stefano. We're a great trio.'

He came up close to me and said, 'Do you come from Rome?'

'Me—no, I've only been in Rome a short time.'

'So you haven't known Anna Drei very long?'

'Just a few days.'

'Is that all? And you became friends straight away?'

'We aren't friends. Perhaps we shall be—but it takes time.'

'That's right,' said Antonio. 'It's the same with me really, with Gianni and Stefano . . . perhaps we shall be friends, but it takes time.'

He stopped; he was rather embarrassed. I looked at him. 'What's up?' I said.

'What's up is that . . . I was wondering, if us two, you and I, will become friends.'

'Sure—I don't see why not.'

'Girls are so difficult,' Antonio said, 'they're so odd.'

'So are boys.'

'I don't think so,' countered Antonio. 'I think they're quite straightforward. If I like a girl, I like her.'

'Me too—if I like a boy, I like him.'

I looked at Antonio and laughed. I didn't dislike him—far from it. I liked putting my

hands on his shoulders. 'What broad shoulders,'
I said.

Then Antonio laughed too, but nervously, and
the tic at the corner of his mouth was more pro-
nounced. So we kissed, but he soon broke away.
He said Anna might come in.

'If Anna finds me here you'll see what'll happen.'

'What do you expect to happen? I'll tell her—
I'll tell her we kissed.'

'Good for you—you do that. There'll be an
almighty row.'

'Anna's not my mother—she's not my mother
or my father either. I do what I like.'

'So do I—but I steer clear of Anna.'

'Do you know her very well?'

'I've known her for a year.'

'Have you kissed her too?'

Antonio said he hadn't. He said I was mad, and
then he went away. Left alone I began to wonder
why I'd kissed Antonio. He was just another boy:
it could easily have been his friend Gianni or
Stefano. He didn't interest me in the least; his
mouth was like Mario's, with that taste of milk
and tobacco and toothpaste and eau-de-Cologne.
It struck me that perhaps Mario was kissing some
girl—there were several girls in our *pensione* in
the Piazza di Pietra, he only had to call them.
Just as I kissed Antonio, I thought, Mario might
be kissing some girl. Might be kissing, might be
kissing, I kept thinking, and in my mind I saw
Mario with his arms round a girl.

I wanted to get myself into a state; I kept saying kiss, kiss a girl, but I didn't get into a state, I wasn't a bit bothered that I'd kissed Antonio, nor that Mario might be kissing a girl, nor that I'd left Mario—in fact, I wasn't a bit bothered about any man in the world.

I sat thinking for a long time. Then Anna came in.

'Anna,' I said, 'I kissed Antonio today and he kissed me.'

'Good,' said Anna. 'And then?'

'Then he went away.'

'I kissed him once too, but he didn't do anything for me. He's a little lamb.'

'But he was sweet,' I said.

'Then he'll go sour,' Anna said.

She began sewing a stocking. I could see her face bent over her work, her eyes intent on what she was doing. Then I found I was crying and Anna gave me a handkerchief.

XIV

That night I didn't sleep.

I tried to drop off, but then I got up, switched on the light, and read some more of Anna's manuscript.

'If I start thinking', Anna had written, 'I see in my mind all the people from my childhood days. I know each person's face and gestures and way of walking—they're people I know, men and women who knew me when I was a little baby, and others who are my own age or a bit older. In all of them I sense the deep melancholy that dogs each one of us as we go out into the streets, or step out of our houses to go somewhere, put one foot in front of the other, echo with our arms the movements of our bodies, our heads held erect or a little bowed, eyes open, not knowing why we should be going, why the rhythm of our steps should be as it is, why our mouths should speak, our ears hear noises.

'All around I saw houses, high buildings with holes and windows, and there were people in them sleeping and eating, and behind the houses were mountains, and the houses faced the sea, and sometimes there were trees and strange-looking plants with flowers.

'If people greeted me, I greeted them back.

' "It's Anna," they used to say, "it's Anna."

'I used to laugh about this—what did it mean to be Anna, I used to think. Others were called by other names, girl friends of mine, and also boys who had tender mouths with scarcely a shadow round them . . . I was attracted towards the boys, without knowing it.

'In the evening, when I was a big girl, I used to go for walks with my girl friends—little groups of us; we used to look in shop windows, or talk about funny little things that had happened to us. There was a rather narrow street that led to the old part of the city: it wound like a thin worm between the houses with ancient portals and figures in relief. It was a lively street, with shops that sold fish and umbrellas and string and religious objects, and there were all sorts of people, and different languages and nationalities.

'For me it was an in-between period. I had gone from childhood to adolescence, and now it was as if I had stopped and was waiting; and if my girl friends talked about woman's things, I kept out of it, I edged away because I thought it was too soon for such things.

'And yet my body was creeping up on me; it was changing, as I could see quite clearly when secretly at home I looked at myself naked in the mirror. I was afraid, I touched horrible swellings, I watched my spotless flesh grow vulgar hair, and I was almost seized with vomiting, my stomach would go taut with nausea.

'One of my girl friends became my confidante. I used to go with her into the room behind her father's photographic shop. It was a big room where we were often left alone. It had enormous screens painted with flowers and birds on branches, and seascape backgrounds with fishes and corals. My friend was called Elsa and she was about thirteen. She had marvellous black eyes, a round face and a small mouth. I can see her now as she was that winter, when she came out of school with her little light-coloured fur coat, rather short, and a beret on the side of her head, and a tight white jumper.

'In the room behind the shop there was hardly ever much light—only very few people came to be photographed—so that Elsa and I used to talk in a corner about our affairs, about the boys we'd seen in the street, and how some of them had looked at us. Slowly, as time went on, she and I began talking about secret things—at first we were afraid of being overheard, and then bit by bit we got bolder and took off our clothes behind the screens with flowers on them, Elsa angrily taking off her white sweater, and me my dress, and

53

we used to compare our two bodies in minute detail, and then throw ourselves into each other's arms, trembling with cold.

'I had been ill for a few days when Elsa died— it was my mother who told me. The funeral passed right under our windows.

'After Elsa I met a boy.

'Really I wasn't interested in him: I was more or less forced to meet him by some of my scheming girl friends. For some time he had been sending me letters through a certain Laura, who was in a higher form than me; Laura was a very well-built girl, with a trace of hair on her upper lip, and eyebrows that met over her nose. She used to follow the little love affairs of us girls in the lower forms.

'She would bring me the letters hidden in a book. She took a malicious pleasure in watching me read them, and she used to write in reply—all sugar-sweet passionate stuff, packed with exclamation marks.

'This boy went to another school. He wore glasses, and behind them his eyes seemed good and imploring. He wrote that he loved me, that I was his life, and things like that. I said I loved him too.

'So I had to go to my first date with him on a road right out in the outskirts towards the hills.

'I went with Laura and some other girls who pumped me with advice on how I should behave, what I ought to say and do. They left me at the end of the road and went to wait behind the last houses, where I was supposed to meet up with them again half an hour later.

'When I started walking on my own I was absolutely terrified and my legs were shaking. In my mind I saw my childhood days, the lovely games I had played, that sense of wonder when I discovered the sky and the sea, and then my changing way of speech . . . and then when I grew up I had nothing left, not even my mother realised I had changed, and she grew apart from me.

'He was a tall boy, when I saw him close up— and slim, like a nice human tree.

'He had the beginnings of a moustache, and nails that were very long and clean and shaped. He led me by the hand through the shrubs and undergrowth up on the hills: we followed some paths into a thick dark wooded area where we sat on a tree-trunk.

'He began talking about love, he held me tight and kissed me on the mouth; then his hands groped under my clothes, and I sat there, still and rigid. Only when his nails scratched my flesh did I jerk out of my daze. I shouted, I called him names. He dropped his glasses, and I took my chance to run away.

'And then I wandered over the hills, oblivious of the other girls who were anxiously waiting to hear what had happened; I felt weightless, dreamy, and even happy.

'It was that strange feeling I have sometimes

when I belong to nature, and nature belongs to me. All round me were leaves and branches and shrubs, whole families of insects, stones, little streams, and I was the only thinking creature among them, with a divine spark in my heart.

'They were rather undulating hills, rugged, with no trace of man, and between them were darkish little valleys, full of mystery.

'It all belonged to me; above me was the sky, that mass of blue that I was breathing in.

'It was beautiful. In later years I lived again the sensations of that afternoon, of being alone among millions of invisible beings, of feeling within my body a strength that was unique, something precise and joyful, and the horror of a man's nails groping for me.'

XV

'Unfortunately I soon discarded such ideas. Days passed and became months, then years. I used to talk to myself in subterranean dialogues when nobody was listening.

'Anna: "Look how I've changed. But all around me I've seen things stay put. I'm amazed at myself."

'The other Anna: "Everything changes, the flowers swell with pollen, and the creatures of the earth are reborn through suffering."

'Anna: "I don't feel like going on living. I shy away from human contact, I'd like my flesh and bones to freeze like the snow up on the mountains."

'The other Anna: "I have blood in me that flows, as red as fire, and suddenly it flares up. Everything has the taste of amorous madness. Alone, I am incomplete, I have no ambitions, I'm useless and vile."

'So I and the other Anna became one and the same. Both of us kept quiet, and if the other Anna talked sometimes, I was the one who gave in.

'For the rest it was just fine—touching the bottom, drowning in the abyss, and then being born again with a richness that had the flavour of the sun, even if there wasn't any sun. I had fleeting glimpses of different countries; I was curious about what there was to see, but it all came down to the same thing. If, for instance, I went somewhere (it might be some foreign city) I breathed an atmosphere that was gay or dismal, the streets might be bright, or else there were dark buildings that made everything look gloomy, or the roofs were all red and made things look cheerful . . . places varied, but after a sudden flood of joy I soon became aware of how useless it all was, as if the mark of dissatisfaction had been branded on my heart. And then I would wander around, seized with fits of despair . . . and still the fountains gushed water, and through the revolving doors of night clubs people were sucked in and spewed out, and often in the shop windows I saw carnival masks.

'Once I found myself in an almost Nordic setting where there was a river, and houses with steep roofs, and churches with tall spires, and the carnival was in full swing. The people lined the streets to watch the floats go past, and they were all wearing enormous masks over their faces, and the children were talking a foreign language.

58

'What a desolate city that was.

'My heart was wounded by the feeling of madness in those streets milling with people. Those pieces of coloured paper, those carnival sweets, and the oranges being thrown about: in that vast city I felt I was a bad, depraved woman, with that boy's nails groping under my clothes up on the hill back in my little country, and I shouted and shouted, I broke down in tears, I trembled with fever, I retched at the thought of food down my throat, at wine to make me drunk, at the wretched machine of my body expelling filth from my belly, that monstrous engine.

'I longed for the angels I'd seen in my mother's books . . . blue and pink angels with white feathery wings; they flew over the clouds, and their feet didn't touch the earth.

'If I were an angel there would always be someone to drive me down again.

'If I flew there would be someone to say it was all fantasy.

'You men, you have the power to imprison the hearts of young girls.

'You send them plunging where it's all darkness.

'Where there are no more of those memories and those talking dolls we used to play with.

'One Anna says that men are the gods of this absurd gift of life. The other Anna says that lies are the only truth in this world.'

XVI

'It was the lights that gave me happiness.

'I would be writing in the evening on odd scraps of paper, and outside the scene would be all lit up . . . oh, then I would be completely happy.

'Lights, lights—a window, a street lamp, a neon sign, car headlights: I used to laugh at myself—mad, stupid Anna, where are you, Anna? What's happened to you? Why are you writing, what have you got in your head? Yours is only the story of what you have inside you—it's subtle, it would escape even the shrewdest observer.

'Yours is only the sickness of all the invisible fibres of existence; they are the strings that control your arms and legs, the motive behind your actions.

'There's someone who commands you.

'He lives outside you and outside everybody.

'You will never discover him.

'It was the lights that consoled me.

'They were like friends to me.

'If I had a man with me, and he was asleep, I might hear his breathing, and I would be far away, I would become again the Anna who went for walks with her mother, like the day we bought the little brown duck.

'Pretty little creature—Anna was fond of it, she liked to touch its feathers, to bath it in a tub of water. My mother and I bought the duck one summer day; there were lots of them but I chose the smallest, the one with little feet. My mother was with me, and her voice was full of love for living creatures.

'My mother: "You're a little girl, and you have the seed of great and eternal things within you. God spoke to me the night you were born."

'Anna: "It was cold when I was born, Mother. That icy cold has stayed in my heart."

'My mother: "Fire melts glaciers. And snow brings back life when it melts in the sun."

'It was the lights that drove out the cold in my veins.

'Sometimes at night I woke up frozen—even my heart had stopped beating. No man's caresses could bring back my strength, and I came to think I was dying.

'But it all passed, it was none of it true: in reality my body was like a beautiful sleepy statue; desires were building up in me, my arms wanted

61

to squeeze, my mouth to bite, my mind laughed as it spun round on its mysterious course.

'If I let myself go, I surrendered completely, I went to pieces, I was shattered, my heart fled and rolled away into the distance—and went off to hide in unheard-of places. And so men were grateful to me; but they didn't know that this wild plunge was a kind of death, that everything in me was contradictory, mad, absurd.

'They laughed perhaps; they battened on my physical and mental ruin: to me they were like octopuses sucking the marrow from my bones; they left me empty and mindless on the edge of precipices.

'There were lots of them, too many of them. They were like precipices where I knew that I could have died, but I didn't yet want to die.

'(The sun, the sun I loved, and running through grass, playing with children—and perhaps I would have some of my own one day, but heaven knew when.)'

XVII

'It was a rainy evening when I met him, and I was still very young.

'I was on my way out for my usual walk through the trees when he came up to me. For a long time I had been expecting him, and it seemed natural to be walking with him.

'He was tall, with fair hair. I began, there and then, to dream of a future with him.

'In my heart there was a feeling of content; I was completely relaxed with him, but we didn't kiss. He bought me some violets from an old woman on the roadside. I felt as if I had reached a turning. His voice brought me sweet joys, I became a little girl again.

'My head was full of magic thoughts and strange visions.

'What a good strong hand it was that held mine. We told each other everything about ourselves: but I told him about only one of the two Annas (the other one had got lost and was dormant), and he fell in love with that heavenly Anna, he was smitten by her.

'So it went on for a long time. The story of those days has no story.

'It must have lasted for years—summers at the seaside, winters in the mountains, and those youthful dreams of a rose-tinted future: the little house with a garden, the gold ring on my finger, and the plans—money didn't come into it—the nursery for our children, and growing old together. Yes, he gave me peace: my face lost its tense look and filled out, my eyes became clear, I quietly blossomed. And yet at night, when I slept alone, and I was waiting for the wedding day (I would be dressed in white, it would be a church wedding, with music and everybody happy), I couldn't sleep.

'I would toss and turn, and keep opening and closing my eyes, and I had a thirst that water couldn't satisfy. After he had quietly said good night to me, he must have lain waiting for the next day so that he could see me again, and if sometimes I slyly worked him up with my caresses, he would be so good and control himself and push me away, because there was time and we had to wait.

'And so, as the seasons came and went, I slowly began to hate him deep down. I would burst into tears and have hysterical fits, and often I longed to be forgiven for hating him, because it

64

seemed such an inhuman thing to be doing.

'By now my whole body was like a taut bow aiming I didn't know where; my body was burning, and sometimes I shouted out and sometimes I fell into long heavy silences like the night.

'And yet I loved him: he was the flower in my desert, he was the only one; I felt humiliated, and I would have liked him to beat me; that adoring voice of his only hurt me, and so did the sweet trusting way he looked at me, and the tender way he put his arms round me yet hardly touched me.

'I don't know what drove me to be unfaithful to him, if that's what it was. It was in the summer, and burning hot in the city, when I went with another man in a small hotel room and I opened myself completely like an insect putting out its wings.

'The other man was small and swarthy, with round piercing eyes, and nasty hands.

'He had been round me like a snake for some time; I still didn't realise he had me in his coils, and then all of a sudden he gripped me tight, and I couldn't escape. They were short sessions in that little room, but I couldn't do without them.

'At the very moment when I took wing, I didn't imagine I was with the other man, but with my only loved one, tall and fair, and it was to him that I called out, him I felt in my flesh and blood, piercing me and giving me strength.

'I was a butterfly with big wings, flecked with gold, and my woman's body was developing areas of heavenly pleasure that I had never thought to exist, and I was drowning.

'The small swarthy man used to be exhausted after those secret meetings, but I would come away having discovered myself.

'As soon as I was outside in the street again my heart swelled with a sense of wonder, and the sun, the warmth on the stones, the water in the sea, the city streets, the people dressed in white—they all seemed to rush to meet me, they seemed created just for me, so that I could see them and enjoy them.

'I had changed: my beauty was complete now, and even my chaste loved one noticed it. Now I loved him in a maternal way, and he rather withdrew into the background; he didn't talk the same way any more about our precious plans for marriage: it was as if I had contemplated a mystery and now carried it written on my forehead . . . and he was about to decipher the writing.

'I don't know now whether all this made me happy, but certainly everything had changed for me; and as I had found a balance between the two beings lurking in my heart, I could well have been happy.

'I had the two Annas within me (the other one often made fun of me and laughed): they dragged me into heaven or hell—as the fancy took them— and heaven and hell were both heaven.

'How can I describe that marvellous time, when I was still so young and I bubbled with enthusiasm

66

about nothing at all. I liked the cars that sped through the streets, the noisy trams and that funny way they had of clattering over crossings. I often wore red or blue; my skin was white and my hair came down to my shoulders.

'One morning I was on my way back from meeting the bad man, and I felt full of strength. I saw my loved one waiting for me in the usual place. It was a deserted road, high above the city, with trees and benches on one side, and on the other side a low wall. Down below, the sparkling houses ran gently down to the sea—they were newly painted in pale colours, with bright green shutters and big white roof gardens.

'I saw him waiting for me, leaning against a tree, looking rather lost, with little branches touching his head; absent-mindedly he was picking off leaves. When he spotted me his face lit up.

'He came towards me. "Darling," he said.

'He told me I was looking beautiful that morning.

'I don't know why "the other Anna" laughed inside me, laughed and shook herself, and then spoke. I, Anna, listened in terror.

' "Do you know where I've been?" the other Anna said.

' "No," he said, "at your place, I suppose."

' "Not at my place," the other Anna said.

' "Where then?"

' "At a man's house."

' "What man?"

' "A man who knows all about me," said the other Anna. Then she explained, "He knows how I cry out when he squeezes me. He makes me beautiful—he's done it again today—and you've noticed it."

'Then my loved one moved away from the tree; he backed away with his arms held out against me and his fingers spread out in horror.

' "Your beauty is a thing from hell," he said.

' "My beauty is a thing from heaven," the other Anna kept saying, walking towards him with eyes glittering and bosom swelling with love—oh, I wanted that fair-haired boy so badly I could have made him go out of his mind.

' "You're lost—like a leaf torn off a branch," he said. "Nothing will save you—and you're destroying me too."

'Then I, Anna, tore myself away from the other Anna and I burst into tears and put my arms round him, and held him tight. But he pushed me away, and then he was on the edge by the wall and below him was just a sheer drop, and I knew I was going to see him fall.

'Why didn't I pull him back?

'Why didn't my nails become hooks in his flesh, why didn't I manage to stop him doing that insane thing?

'I just stood there stunned, with all the breath knocked out of me.'

XVIII

'Tiredness isn't a good enough reason to go on living.

'When I think of the days to come, my heart goes dead. And then, because of my total cowardice, I look forward to any sort of death, as painless as possible.

'I wouldn't know how to do it myself.

'I just wait for it to come from outside.

'If there's a law that governs our actions, and that says everything must be paid for, then I, Anna Drei, will pay one day.

'When that will be, I don't know.

'Perhaps I'm afraid.

'From that far-away city overlooking the sea, I fled that morning. I got to know other cities as I grew older, and always "the other Anna" got the better of me, because the real Anna was dead.

' "The other Anna" is waiting to die.

'But having exceptional vitality, her life will

be long, days will be followed by more days, men by more men.

'What strange skies I saw on my wanderings. One I remember—it was as red as fire, a mass of flames and reddish streaks falling on the countryside. There were mountains in the distance, and I was alone down there, thinking. I know my thoughts were vague and sad: they took me back to my youth, to those sweet memories of early times.

'When he shyly squeezed my arm and talked about us, about how it would be when we were grown up—oh what sweet pipe-dreams.

'Now the skies are heavy; winter imprisons me in its greyness. How tired I am of walking . . . and yet with every step I might still discover marvels —after all, geraniums bloom in window boxes, children suddenly appear in doorways and mothers call them in, and in shop windows dresses fall into beautiful folds, and blue eyes look at me . . . and behind me are all the hosts of the dead and in front of me is the unknown.

'The dead fill the universe with their stench, their bones give off sparks, at night the cemeteries are fields of flowers, the stars descend from the sky, and the dead are cold and fearful.

'We have built our houses on top of the dead.

'In the walls there are fragments of their flesh.

'If I shut myself in a room, the air disappears, and I am terrified they will come and suffocate me.

'But before me lie the days, the heavenly hours, when my mouth will open and speak, my ears hear sounds, when arms will close around my body—this is my only sweet richness.

'I love Anna Drei, I made her; I gave birth to her, my womb brought her forth. I shall be the one to tell her when her heart should cease to beat. Anna Drei is the fantasy of a raging brain, the imagining of a sick mind.

'Anna Drei has no story. She is a creature that runs away and hides.

'My mother used to say, "Humility is the sweetness of human life."

'Anna would reply, "Wings are made for flying, and the world is only a fantasy seen from above."

'So I loved, and so I have learnt to cope. If anyone smiles at me, I smile back; if they hurt me, I hurt them back.

'Yet sometimes I feel so desperate. I would like the roads never to end and my feet to swell as I walk along them, or something to come crashing down on me, on the cage of my body, so that I could be fresh and naked, smelling of flowers.'

XIX

The next morning Anna Drei came up to me. She had just washed her face and she had a strange look . . . her cheekbones seemed a little higher as if she had got thinner all of a sudden. It was early, and I was still reading.

I looked at her. I think I must have looked at her in an odd way—perhaps I stared a bit. It was as if she had stripped off her clothes in front of me.

'Don't read any more,' she said.

'I've nearly finished it.'

'It's not true—any of it.'

'I thought maybe it was all just a story.'

Anna started laughing. 'I'd like to know,' she said, 'what you mean by true. I always feel I'm being true to myself in my stories.'

I threw the manuscript down on the bed, and the pages scattered.

'I'm going,' I said, 'I'm going back to Mario.'

'You as well—you're just like all the others,' said Anna.

'Yes, me as well. So long as you're different— that's all that matters, isn't it?'

'Oh, I'm different all right,' said Anna.

She was silent for a bit, looking out of the window. 'It's raining,' she said.

'I'm not scared of getting wet.'

So I started packing my case. Anna helped me get my stuff together; she folded my clothes and picked up my shoes.

'You don't know why you want to leave here.'

'I know perfectly well.'

'Try to explain then.'

I tried to explain, but it was difficult, I couldn't find the words or the reasons. 'Tell me,' I said, 'why did you make me come here?'

'You came—nobody forced you.'

'That's true—I came.'

I looked round—at our things, the books, the stockings on the chairs. We were a couple of tramps.

'Where's your mother?' asked Anna.

'A long way away,' I replied.

Again there was a silence; then Anna opened up the case, took out my stuff and threw it all over the place.

I let her do it. Then I said, 'What's got into you, Anna?'

'I can't tell you. Whatever it is, I've written it all down.'

'About that boy—was it true, about that boy up on the road?'

Anna said that yes, it was true. She also said she had seen him again a few years later.

'How could you see him again?' I said.

'I saw him, it was him, only a bit younger.'

'But it must have been some other boy, not him. He was dead.'

'It was him but younger,' said Anna. 'It was one afternoon. He went by on a bicycle and I called out to him. I was walking along a road I didn't know; it was summer-time, and he was wearing shorts and a striped jersey—the one he often wore. I called him by his name. "Paolo," I said, "Paolo." He stopped and got off. He was tall and fair, and his skin was so pale that afternoon. "Anna," he said, "it's you." We went off together and sat on the grass at the side of the road.'

'It's impossible,' I said, interrupting her.

'We said we loved each other,' Anna went on, 'but he couldn't remember what had happened. He didn't know what I'd said to him that morning. What's more, I didn't know myself either.'

'But where is he now? Where's he gone?'

'I went away—he didn't. He asked me to stay, he begged me very sweetly. He talked about the scenery round there, which was very beautiful, and he said we'd be happy. The grass was long, and there were poppies growing in the corn.'

'I like those sort of places too,' I said, 'but I've never seen them.'

'You can see all the things that I see, only you must let yourself go.'

For the first time she had used the familiar *tu*, like a sister. I put my arms round her. 'Forgive me, Anna,' I said.

'My mother,' said Anna, 'is buried a long way away. My mother really loved me.'

She went and got the bottle of *grappa*, and poured some out for both of us. '*Grappa*,' she said, 'like the carters drink.'

Then she smoked a cigarette. She said she was going out and asked if I'd like to come too; she said she was fed up with being haunted by memories. 'What I've been saying,' she said, 'it's all pure invention out of this brain of mine.' And she clapped her hand to her head. Then she threw open the window, and the rain came in. We went out on to the roof garden and looked out. The rain beat in our faces and down on our hair. Rome lay shrouded in a light grey mist, like a fairy city.

'Rome, I hate it,' Anna said.

She said there were moments when she hated it, when she hated all the cities in the world—when she found it repugnant to be living on this earth.

She picked up a page of her manuscript, and read it out. ' "One summer I went swimming in the sea. I went right out where the water was deep. I tried to see what was down on the bottom. The bottom was green."

'Winter, spring . . .' she said, 'it'll be some time before summer comes.'

Besides, she said, she didn't care about summer either. And she said everything she'd written just made her laugh, and she was a mediocre writer.

She took out the whole manuscript, and together we tore it up; we threw it down from the roof garden, and the rain swallowed it up. The pieces of paper floated down on to the roofs and window-sills.

'If I want to write, I write really beautiful things,' Anna said. 'But when I've written them I don't know what to do with them.'

Then she said, 'I wonder why we have to do certain things. Now, for instance, we're looking out at the rain, and it doesn't mean a thing to us.'

'It means something to me,' I said.

It really did mean something to me: the rain gave me a sense of freedom, a feeling of joy. I felt miles away from everything. I was thinking of Mario, alone in that room in the Piazza di Pietra. I was miles away from Anna.

'What a little woman,' Anna said.

'Little woman—who?' I said.

'You,' Anna said, 'you of course.'

I slapped her, and we went rolling on the floor. We lashed out at each other like wild things, and I nearly tore her clothes off.

I felt a bitter sensation, hitting her and being hit by her; and I could feel the rain soaking us. I bit Anna's arm and a sweetish taste came into my mouth, a taste of woman. I was filled with horror.

XX

That night I went to Mario's and slept with him.

It was late when I got into his bed, and Mario was asleep.

I snuggled up against him, and woke him up.

'Mario, I've come back.'

He said a dirty word. 'She didn't have very good taste,' he said.

'What taste—who?'

'That Anna—Anna Drei.'

I said he was wrong, that it wasn't true at all. Mario began laughing, laughing in that hysterical way of his that went right through my head.

'Stop laughing,' I said.

'I'll laugh as much as I like.'

He was hurting me, he was pressing me down on the bed.

'You're heavy,' I shouted. 'You're hurting me.'

But he was hurting me on purpose: I could feel his body on mine like a block of stone, and his mouth on my face. 'You're slobbering all over me,' I shouted.

'Like a dog,' he said.

I don't remember when we went to sleep . . . something had changed in me too. I was no longer the girl from the Villa Celimontana; contemptible creature that I was, Anna had me in torment.

Those pages of her manuscript, my God—torn up, thrown down from the roof garden—how desperate she must have been. What a useless way of life. I felt as if my body counted for nothing in the great world around me; what a little thing I must be among the mountains, seas and deserts! And Mario was a man I didn't love.

I found myself thinking about Anna's boy; I pictured him—so tall and fair, with gentle manners, and he smiled at me from his paradise of flowers.

'Why didn't you love me?' I said.

'Because you didn't know me then.'

He looked at me with those eyes I hadn't seen before; Anna had said they were blue. He didn't speak; he just smiled faintly, rather dreamily.

'Why didn't I meet you on earth?'

(Mario stirred in the bed . . . I was surely dreaming. Mario was alive, I was alive, and Anna's boy was dead.)

I asked myself why we die. Anna's boy opened his mouth and said, 'We die when the seasons grow old in us, the flowers fade, and the streams have no more water.'

And then I called Mario—I woke him up again. 'What's up?' he said. 'What's happening?'

He took me in his arms and kissed me, but I couldn't stand it; I pushed him away—that big live body of his disgusted me.

XXI

The next morning I went out alone.

I walked back along the road where I had walked with Anna the night when there was a moon. I bought some dried figs—they were threaded on a piece of cane bent in a circle. I tore off each fig; they were good and tasty.

I ate and thought. It wasn't very cold; the city seemed to be shrugging off the cold.

I thought about life for girls. I thought about Anna's life, about mine, about the lives of other girls, and I felt the dissatisfaction and sadness of each one. I thought too, of my mother—she was far away and different from me: every mother is different from the creature she gives birth to.

Time had come between us and our mothers; there had been years of pain, and important changes, wars had altered the places we loved, cataclysms had swept through our minds, and there was no trace of our childhood left to us.

Yet it was lovely when we were children, dreaming about those sweet things of life.

Anna said so too; she wrote it, she could remember the Queen on the elephant and what she said.

The Queen used to say, 'Waiting for what must happen consoles us for the passing time. The future is our island of flowers.'

When we were children we had such lovely games. When we knocked down the houses we'd built with our toy bricks we built them up again; when our dolls' eyes came out there was someone to put in new ones.

I was moved by those faraway memories; I walked along, thinking, and a faint gleam of hope lit up inside me, and told me to hold on and I would be strong again.

Life was sad—full of loneliness; that was why I had Mario, and he had me, that was why I had met Antonio, and he talked to me about the girl from Terni . . . that was why Anna had everybody and nobody.

But we weren't happy—I wasn't, nor was Anna, nor Mario, nor Antonio . . . nor lots of others.

I sensed that something was gnawing at our hearts, torturing us; it wasn't something I could pin down, but it was sharp and cruel.

I walked through the streets of Rome, I walked along eating figs; my teeth chewed, my body was strong; above me was the air, and on all sides were people passing.

I watched those people and in each of them I seemed to see my own dissatisfied human nature, and Anna's; like me and like Anna, those people were asking for something, they were looking upwards, or searching in the bowels of the earth . . . but they were receiving no reply.

XXII

Anna wrote me a letter.

Antonio brought it to me, while Mario was out.

I kissed him. It didn't mean a thing to me, but I did it because in life you do so many useless things—and they're necessary in order to appreciate the right and useful things when they come along. . . . But the awful thing is they don't come along.

Antonio kissed me back. He said he'd thought about me a lot since our first meeting. I laughed, I reminded him of his girl, and he said he hadn't heard from her.

Then he said, 'Read Anna's letter.'

'I'll read it later.'

'She was very odd, was Anna. She called me in to bring you this letter and she kissed me on the mouth like you did.'

He seemed put out about telling me this; it annoyed him to think he was being used as a guinea pig. He was a shy awkward boy, and he didn't have much personality. I sent him away.

I opened the letter. 'You see,' wrote Anna, 'I don't want to see you ever again. Any more than I want to see anyone. I made a mistake getting to know you, just as I've done with all the others. My real strength is the marvellous feeling of solitude that I have, of talking all alone with my heart. I have everything I could desire—I don't have to look outside. I'm complete in myself; too often I've made the mistake of asking men for what I thought I lacked. But instead they gave me nothing—I was the one who gave something. Sometimes I'm gripped by a kind of apathy, I almost go into a trance. I spend whole days on my bed in a sort of deep drowsy state; my body ceases to exist, my spirit wanders restlessly.

'And then I feel supremely happy.

'It's as if my arms and legs put out roots and sprouted leaves, as if birds nested in my trunk. This has been going on for a long time, but I don't talk to anybody about it, it's one of my secrets. You've never seen me like that; to you I've seemed a different Anna. But you've always seemed different to me from what you really are. I realised that when we were on the floor out on the roof garden.

'We were hurting each other and all the evil of the world was on us two—I who have known it, and you who have yet to know it.

'Once, a long way from here, I saw a big frozen

84

lake. The countryside all round was bare and sprinkled with snow, and you could see the earth peeping through. The lake was shut in on itself, as proud and menacing as a god. It was covered over with ice, its lovely water had disappeared. I feel like that lake: ice grips my heart and deadens the spark of life left in me.

'Underneath I suffer, underneath I cry out, I ask for help. You don't know what it means not to be able to reach the surface.

'People were looking at the lake, and a few tried to walk on it: the ice swallowed them up.

'I don't venture deep into myself; I stay outside, I amuse myself, futile things seem to interest me, the silly things that occupy so many people. And yet the contradiction is always there in me. I envy the simple-minded, the little children who don't yet know what human nature is, and look forward to growing up.

'I often think of death—you've read that in my manuscript; it's my consolation, thinking about it.

'It must be very sweet to die.

'When I've no more hope, and when at certain times of the day I dread the future, I think what very subtle forms of death I might choose. Maybe I don't mean a real bodily death, but the negation of all the senses, the annihilation of this filthy flesh of mine.

'I look at myself in mirrors; I take off my clothes, I lift up my hair, I examine my body—I'm so desperately woman.

85

'Horrible female organs, monstrous mouths that open and ask to be fed. I feel I'm sacrificing all human dignity to them, sacrificing my whole self just to let loose that brief pleasure that sends me plunging. And then I'm left with a taste like rotting flesh: it's me reduced to that, a nothingness, a poor lava.

'But it was lovely running, when I was a little girl.

'I won all the races. My mother and brothers used to enjoy watching me come in first, as light as a cloud, and all the other boys and girls panting behind.

'I didn't know then what was going to become of me; in those days I lived in bliss.

'And you too—you don't know why you've grown up. Your bones have changed, like mine; arms, legs, everything has been transformed—your hands are no longer the ones you had before, nor your eyes, and you have a different skin. The little girl from those childhood days—where did she go, where did the others go? I searched for them, the boys of those days, the girls who played those games, and even some who had the same Christian name as me didn't recognise me, and I didn't recognise them. They seemed to have grown ugly, pale, preoccupied with worldly things instead of running races or watching butterflies.

'And so I repeat myself, monotony goes everywhere with me, I'm always thinking of the same things, it hurts me to remember my poor childhood years. If I tell a man how much it makes me suffer, he laughs at what he calls these "fantasies", he opens his arms, he says he can console me, show me the right road.

'But perhaps I've never really known a man.

'Perhaps I've forgotten them all, I forget them as soon as they've left my room or I theirs.

'Sometimes I kiss young boys; they have lips as fresh as children, their eyes are still clear.

'I kissed a boy down at the sea one year. He was slim, with skin as fine as silk. We swam together, and he held me tight in the sea.'

I stopped reading, and wrote a couple of lines to Mario, saying I was going back to Anna's.

I walked up the stairs of her *pensione* with a feeling of joy. Anna was at home.

'I'm here,' I said.

'Good,' said Anna.

'I read your letter,' I said. 'You said you didn't want to see me ever again.'

'I'm seeing you now,' Anna said.

XXIII

And so time passed.

It was still winter, but spring was drawing close and on some mornings the whole city seemed to glitter. If Anna and I went out into the streets, we were speechless with wonder.

Anna had said very little since my return to her place; her face had a calm expression, she was very nice to me, she was a sweet kind girl and it was a pleasure to be with her. We used to wake up fairly early; the cold water gave us a sense of starting afresh, and when we opened the window for a few moments the air that came in smelled new and sweet. We would go downstairs and buy ourselves some food, and then walk through the streets till we were tired.

Sometimes, when we went out by the Porta San Giovanni, we walked along the Via Appia Antica. There were tombs down there, and fabulous remains of buildings, and green fields everywhere,

88

and no one to bother us . . . and Anna became her real self again. She told me about her life, about things that had happened in the woods, and the first trip she went on with her brothers, the snow on the mountains. I used to talk too, but I hadn't had such an eventful life and I was rather embarrassed and I often fell back on talking about Mario, the only man for me.

'Why do you talk about him if you don't love him?' Anna used to say. And then, 'You lived with him because it's the thing to do these days, but deep inside you were sorry you did it.'

I said nothing to these insinuations of hers; I was ashamed at having so little imagination, silly girl that I was, ending up with a boy like that.

'But he gave you pleasure?' Anna would insist.

Yes, he had given me pleasure; and then I would talk about him, talk at great length about him; I would undress Mario in front of her, and there we would see him—his fine straight body, his shoulders, his chest, his arms, and those slim legs of his that gripped, and his hands that hurt.

Anna would beg me to stop, and I would do as she asked; but it always left something between us, an area of dark shadows. We would feel strangers, walking well apart, each of us stopping to look at different things, I a tree, Anna another tree, I a stone, Anna another stone. There were some curious things down there—ancient carvings, inscriptions on stones—and we used to try to make them out. Anna would laugh: she couldn't do it.

She would say, 'Don't let's talk about men— they lead us astray. They can even turn us against each other.' She would look up at the sky, take off her beret and loosen her hair, and I would look at her, at her face, and feel full of melancholy.

One evening we felt depressed, so we went out along the Via Appia Antica. It was dark and we walked a long way. Suddenly Anna made me turn up a path that led into the fields.

I stumbled along and nearly fell two or three times. Anna went on ahead, moving with surprising sureness, and sometimes she gave me her hand. I was opening my eyes wide and staring into the darkness, but I couldn't see a thing. All of a sudden we turned right, then left.

There was an open space, bathed in harsh light as if it was floodlit. I couldn't make out where the light was coming from. I saw the skeleton of a house, a high frightening wall like a mouth with the teeth missing . . . all the windows were out.

The house had been completely blackened by fire. Opposite, on the other side of the bare white patch of ground, was a long low hut with a big open door. The light didn't penetrate beyond that doorway: it stopped on the threshold, and inside there was darkness, grim and thick, like the darkness all around.

Anna let go of my hand and began to run. I shouted out, but she had already disappeared.

XXIV

An extraordinary creature, was Anna.

She was capable of anything. I remember how she nursed me after that incident in the fields. We never spoke of what had happened, and Anna didn't give me any explanation. I was ill, I had a fever, I was bathed in cold sweat; Anna wiped my forehead, gave me water with lemon to wet my lips; she changed my vest, and the pillow, and sat beside me.

Antonio came to see us, and brought me some oranges. He said there was a lot of flu about. His sister in Terni had written and said so, and his sister's girl friend had added a postscript . . . she had been ill, too.

'Girls, when they're sick,' said Antonio, 'are like little tigers.'

'Little tigers—what do you mean?' I said.

'In a trap,' said Antonio.

We laughed—Antonio was funny. But Anna

told him he knew nothing about tigers, he wasn't a tamer. Antonio admitted he wasn't, but he said he'd be glad to learn. Anna said that our room wasn't a circus. Then she sent him off, and he went out crestfallen. After that Anna read to me out of a book, and I fell asleep.

I was ill for a few more days; when I got up the sun was shining brilliantly, and it was already warm.

I looked at myself in the mirror and I had changed. My face had got even thinner, my eyes were sunken, my lips very pale; I was frail, my legs wouldn't support me. And yet I was up, the fever had gone—that was a victory in itself. Then I phoned Mario. I asked him to come and see me —Anna was going out that afternoon; I hadn't seen Mario for I don't know how long. He said he wasn't interested in seeing me, he wasn't interested in women.

So I stayed alone; I moved restlessly about the room, and picked up a book, then a magazine, then another book; I rifled through a shelf and found a sheet of paper with Anna's handwriting, which I read. She had probably written it quite recently, because I hadn't seen it before.

'She intrigues me', wrote Anna. 'She gives me that subtle mysterious sense of things that are beyond my reach. She's like me: I catch her in my gestures, in certain movements I thought belonged to me. She looks round and observes the same way as I do—like me, she seems a bit uncertain about things, but she doesn't miss much.

'I don't know why I told her to come here. She asked me why herself, once. We aren't attracted to each other physically—in fact we shy away from each other. There's an instinctive revulsion, and each of us is terrified the other will realise it. When we undress we're almost afraid of each other, our nakedness seems monstrous and utterly vulgar; we'd like to be as smooth and clean as young babies. The blood that soils us, and that purifies our bodies, makes us all one in its regular cycle—disgusting thing that it is.

'Sometimes I find she's thinking the same thoughts as me. Dark sad thoughts.

'And yet I'm fond of her; it's not affection, like a woman for a man, or a woman for another woman. It's something else. There was a time when I had the same fondness and loving patience for myself.

'I'd like to lavish the same care on some little flower in a pot—perhaps a primula, or a daisy, or a geranium. In fact I'll buy one. It'll be lovely looking after a flower with her.

'I need to believe in something. Even if it's only that one sort of manure will keep the leaves of my flower fresh while another will give the roots long life in the earth in the pot.

'I have no roots, and yet my feet get a hold wherever they touch. I don't know whether the other Anna has any—I must find out.

'I don't know yet who the other Anna is, or

93

where she comes from—and I haven't asked her. What little she's told me, she'll only have made up, the same way as I do.'

Here she had come to the end of the sheet of paper. I put it back where I'd found it. When Anna came in she was carrying a primula in a pot.

'A primula—why?' I said, pretending to be surprised.

'I just saw it as I was passing—there were lots of them.'

'All like this one?'

'Not like this one. This one's different.'

'It's beautiful,' I said, 'beautiful and green. I'll give it a little water.'

I watered it: the earth drank the water. Anna watched me from a corner of the room, not moving.

But I stopped watering the plant; my head was aching, and the water was brimming over the pot.

XXV

That night we talked for a long time about lots of things; Anna told me what she had done in the afternoon.

'I went out and I didn't know where to go.'

'I phoned Mario.'

'What did you say to him?'

'I said I wanted to see him.'

'What did he say?'

'He didn't feel like it.'

We were silent for a bit. Then Anna said, 'Today my body feels like lead. It was hot out in the street—not at all like winter. My clothes were sticking to me and I felt uncomfortable. I was walking along and I couldn't find anything I liked. My feet were burning—and how grey everything was. I don't know why they make the streets so grey. I was thinking today of making them blue, or pink, or white, but I didn't have the colours— in any case there were too many streets.'

Her voice sank into silence; I didn't know what to say. Just then somebody knocked on the door. I went and opened it, and Mario came in.

'Good evening,' he said, 'I changed my mind.'

He looked round, then he put several bottles on the little table.

'I've brought something to drink.'

'We were just going to bed,' I said.

'That's no reason for not drinking,' Mario said. He seemed casual and relaxed. Anna was watching him, and I felt uneasy.

'If you wanted to see me, we can leave it till tomorrow. It's too late now.'

'Early or late, it doesn't matter. Now's all right for me.'

'I don't know if it's all right for Anna.'

Then Anna spoke. 'It makes no difference to me,' she said.

Mario took off his coat, opened a bottle and gave us each a glass of cognac. It wasn't good. Anna said *grappa* was better, so we drank some to taste the difference.

Then we stretched out; Mario stretched out too.

I don't know what Anna was thinking—certainly our thoughts were as light as feathers. At any rate I was thinking about some games we used to play in the country, when I used to hide in the corn with the other children. Their skin had a smell of young animals.

Mario switched off the light and a vague glimmer came in through the windows. Anna told us that a

96

few months before some witches had come in through the window.

'There were two of them, dressed in green and yellow. One pulled my hair, and the other one was laughing.'

Mario said witches didn't exist any more. I said perhaps it had been Antonio dressed up as a witch. Mario asked who was Antonio. We told him.

Then the conversation sagged; in the silence each of us was fighting against a tense feeling of emotion. I put my head on Mario's chest and he touched my hair.

I could hear Anna's breathing, and it upset me.

Mario stretched out his hand and lightly touched her face.

I sensed Mario's movement in the dark, and I sensed that Anna didn't draw away.

XXVI

I wasn't jealous, though I was suspicious now
when Anna went out. I couldn't wait for her at
home any more, quietly reading a book or going
on to the roof garden to enjoy some sunshine. I
was convinced that Anna was seeing Mario at his
place, and the thought gnawed at me. Mario hadn't
been to see us again; he had phoned me once to say
he was very busy—and I'd heard nothing more.
Anna never talked about him; she kept on going
out and coming in again, just as she'd always done.
Sometimes we went out together, and yet I knew
something in our life had changed.

It was as if we had slipped into two opposite
corners, and our efforts to come together were no
use.

I watched Anna and Anna watched me.

With our eyes we gave each other such looks.

If we stayed at home in the afternoon it was
difficult to find anything to talk about, so we often

went to the cinema, or the theatre, places where there were people and noise. Once I went to Mario's place but he wasn't there. I left him a note, I put it by the bed, but he didn't reply. I looked round my old room with a tight feeling in my heart: it was squalid, there wasn't a single flower there, the curtains hadn't been put back, the rug in front of the mirror had disappeared. I looked out of the window and saw the usual scene: down below the same little balcony, beyond it a roof, then a roof garden, then another roof with clumps of weed in the gutters, and the outlines of the houses marking out the streets running through below. I looked round the room: shirts and jackets and trousers in the cupboard, behind the bed some blue socks which still needed washing, a raincoat stuffed in a drawer, some dirty old combs, a greasy hairbrush. I quickly tidied up, but I was afraid Mario would come in and catch me with his things. Then I gloomily went away.

Those days weren't, in fact, very important. There seemed to be a lull in everything. Even the winter—which by then was merging into spring and bringing the first sunshine and blue skies—seemed to be waiting for a definite sign before it disappeared altogether. It was the same with the people I knew: they were unsure, they wouldn't say anything, and Anna seemed shut up in herself, her face showed no emotion, no expression.

Every day she got up, and washed, and dressed,

and spoke to me in the same voice. Sometimes I got a peep behind her show of calmness, but she quickly closed up, a question of a second or so . . . one or two evenings when she threw herself trembling on the bed, or when she looked in the mirror and her eyes dilated.

How lovely Anna was at that time! I'd never seen her look so lovely.

I don't know where she got that mysterious pallor; her flesh seemed to be drained of blood, like an expanse of cold marble, and her hands were cold and light. I would have liked her to talk to me, as we had once talked to each other about everything going on inside us, in our hearts. My own heart was heavy because I didn't know whom to confide in.

I hadn't got Mario any more; I hadn't got Anna any more.

XXVII

Deep down I couldn't bear being alone.

I had often put on a show of being able to cope with the world, but as for living in isolation so that I could think and gain experience—that had always been a load of nonsense; I realised this now that I felt abandoned, and when I came back home after long walks it was depressing not to have anyone to listen to me.

Sometimes I told myself I'd leave Anna and go back to Mario, but I soon realised there was no point in leaving Anna and going back to Mario.

I don't know whether I ever loved Mario; when Anna had forced me to think about it, I had said no, that I didn't love him.

Anna wanted me to think about things seriously, but Mario wasn't interested in my thoughts. It hurt me that they both neglected me: it seemed such a mean thing, a betrayal.

And yet, sometimes, I knew that Anna was

watching me: as if her eyes, suddenly grown soft, wanted to express something that was paining her. One evening she came up to me, calling me, and wanted us to go out on the roof garden together to see if it was cold. We leaned over the railing: Anna touched me on the shoulder, and when I turned round to ask what she wanted, she said, 'Sorry, I just brushed against you.'

But I knew she had done it on purpose. I said, 'You didn't brush against me, you deliberately touched my shoulder.'

'Touched your shoulder? What are you talking about?'

Then she said it was a starry sky. 'I like to imagine what lies beyond the stars,' she said.

I couldn't imagine what lay beyond them, and Anna didn't tell me. She'd been strange for a long time.

She used to write for hours in her exercise book when we stayed at home; and when she went out alone in the afternoons she took it with her. I was dying to read it.

One day I asked her, 'What are you writing, Anna—another manuscript?'

She shrugged her shoulders. 'I'm writing a letter,' she said.

'A letter? That long?'

'Yes, sure, it's a long one.'

So I didn't ask any more. Each of us could go off without the other protesting; a wall had grown up in our room and divided it in two.

One night Anna didn't come in at all. It was the first time she'd ever stayed out. I waited for her all night. I had made some supper, but it got cold and I didn't eat any myself.

Anna came back late the next day. A few nights later she did the same thing again.

XXVIII

That exercise book Anna had been writing in for some days—I found it late one night, when I came home from the cinema. Anna wasn't in, and I wasn't worrying any more because I'd got used to her being away at nights. The exercise book was right in the middle of the table, and I realised Anna had put it there on purpose. Perhaps I was supposed to read it.

I wanted to satisfy my curiosity when it suited me, so I took my time over everything—in any case there was no hurry. I undressed, I heated some water, I made some tea, I looked at myself a long time in the mirror, I carefully brushed my hair—it had grown during the winter and now it was down to my shoulders. I also watered our primula: it had wilted, the leaves had lost the lovely freshness of the first day.

I went out on to the roof garden: the sky was overcast—perhaps it would rain later on. I heard the bells of the Trinita dei Monti Church striking the hour; they rang out distinctly.

It was horrid of Anna to stay out, I thought; perhaps she was with somebody, a man certainly, and she didn't love him. Or else I imagined her walking the gloomy deserted streets . . . but if she walked about all night the police would want to know what she was doing, where she was going. There were plenty of girls out walking the streets. The police would think she was up to no good.

It was night-time now, the middle of the night.

I shuddered and stepped back into the room: it was well lit, and I slipped into bed.

I had Anna's exercise book with me. It was an ordinary school exercise book, with a coloured cover. Anna, I thought to myself, had a mania for writing down what she had in her heart, and that was fine; of course writing was difficult and a marvellous thing, but why didn't Anna talk to me instead, why didn't she tell me everything instead of being so distant, because maybe we could help each other?

I had lots of things to say as well, but I couldn't write, and if I talked nobody would listen. Once more I put off making a start on the exercise book; I had read Anna's stuff too often, and it always hurt me. I was fed up with torturing my mind and being hurt.

I was straightforward, I was a quiet girl who had lost her way in the world, but I could go back to being a nice good girl. I had talked once to

Anna about my mother, and told her she lived a long way away. I wondered why I had left my mother; she had no idea what I'd been doing, she didn't know anything about Mario or anything else. She thought I was studying and went to classes, she thought I'd soon finish my studies and then go back home; instead of which I hadn't been studying, I was just wasting my time, no classes, no studies, and I'd moved in with Mario, and now with Anna, hanging around with Anna and getting all involved in Anna's affairs.

I felt so angry and sad. I felt like breaking something that would make a lot of noise. I had to make up my mind, I had to give up this life— it was getting me nowhere. I told myself I would leave the next day; I would look for another *pensione* . . . I knew one along by the Porta Pinciana . . . you could see all the trees when you opened the window. I could live very well on my own, I'd get used to it after a time, I wouldn't give my address to anybody, or my phone number, and if Mario went looking for me, let him look—and the same could go for Anna. I didn't like those two any more, I didn't like anybody any more.

I was nearly crying, all alone in that room, in that bed; I was cold, it was night-time and Anna wasn't there, there was no one for me.

Why does this strange apathy come on us women? Why do we let ourselves go like this? What is it that makes us feel so lost, abandoned, so drained of strength?

I really didn't know what it could be.

Earlier that evening I'd been to the cinema, and among all those people I'd felt like screaming; but I stuffed my handkerchief in my mouth, and gradually felt calmer.

Yes, I told myself, I'll start all over again; the next day I wanted to go away, but then, when I had gone away, wouldn't it be just the same? What would I do when I'd gone? I'd go to classes . . . all right, but I didn't give a damn about classes and school, I didn't give a damn about anybody, and Anna didn't give a damn about anybody in the world. And my mother—what was my mother doing? I wasn't even bothered about her—I'd gone away, and she had let me go. How horrible to be reduced to this, I kept telling myself over and over again . . . what a muddle there was in my mind.

If Anna's written a fable, I said to myself, here in her exercise book, then I'll read it now and then I can go to sleep. If it's sunny tomorrow morning everything will be different.

I hoped it was a fable; they were lovely, those fables they used to tell me when I was a little girl. Then I heard rain—it was beating on the roof garden.

I wonder where Anna is? I thought.

At last I opened the exercise book, and just then the door burst open and Mario came running in. He had such a wild look on his face, I thought he'd gone out of his mind.

XXIX

I sat up in bed. I was staggered to see him at that hour, coming in like that without a word of warning.

'What's wrong?' I said. 'What's happened?'

Mario had thrown himself down on the end of the bed; he was trembling and drops of sweat stood at the roots of his hair. Under his soaked raincoat he had on his pyjamas.

'Why aren't you dressed?' I said. 'Why did you go out like that—it's cold and it's raining.'

'It's not raining much,' said Mario.

He said he had run all the way.

'But how did you get in? The street door was locked and so was the door to the *pensione*.'

'I had the keys,' Mario replied.

'The keys? What keys? I've got mine, and Anna's got hers. How could you have them?'

'I've got them,' he said. He dug in his pocket

and showed them to me. They were on a bit of string, like Anna's.

'But those are Anna's,' I said.

Mario said yes they were Anna's.

'Did she give them to you?' I asked, feeling scared. 'But where's Anna? Where's she gone?'

Mario put his hand over my mouth because I was shouting. 'Stop shouting—they'll all hear us.'

I said I wasn't shouting, I'd just raised my voice a bit.

'Where's Anna?' I said. 'If you've got her keys you must have seen her to get them from her.'

'Yes, I got them from her. She had them in her bag.'

'So where's she then?'

'At home.'

'At home—where? At your place?'

I got out of bed and went over to Mario and put my arms round him. 'Why are you shivering? Tell me where you left Anna.'

'I told you—she's at home.'

'Then I'm getting dressed. We'll go and get her—I don't like her being there on her own. Besides, I don't want you to sleep here.'

'I'm not sleeping here—I don't give a damn about sleeping.'

'Why didn't you stay with Anna?'

Suddenly I was very angry: I shook him and tried to hit him. Mario didn't move—he was lying face down.

'You ought to be ashamed of yourself,' I said.

'You've been going with Anna. But I know all about it—I've known for a long time about you two.'

Mario said he hadn't been doing anything with Anna, and he didn't like her either.

'So why did you leave her at your place, in bed? Other times you've slept together.'

Mario said they'd slept together lots of times, but he wasn't in love with any woman in the world. They were all the same: they all went to bed with him, and I had too.

He was so nasty. He made me feel sick, he was so nasty—stupid and nasty.

'Listen, get out of here,' I said. 'I don't want you here.'

'I can't go—I don't know where to go.'

'Go home—you've got your own place.'

'My place—I'm not going back there ever again.'

He shouted that he wouldn't go back there ever again as long as he lived. This time it was my turn to tell him to be quiet—they'd be bound to hear us in the *pensione*. Then Mario suddenly started crying; he was crying and shaking, and biting the bedclothes to muffle the sound.

'Anna,' he said, 'Anna . . .'

'Anna—what? Tell me what's happened. Tell me everything.'

He didn't want to tell me and I didn't understand yet, but then I seemed to sense something. Him in his pyjamas, and the keys he had taken out of her bag. I don't know what made me sense it, but I fell to my knees on the floor, I clenched my fists and pressed them into my eyes; I could feel the invisible presence of Anna, and that secret way she had of talking. I shook myself: my eyes wandered round the room: I saw that Anna's exercise book had finished up on the floor and was lying open at the first page. I didn't so much read the first words—I felt them come thudding into me . . . 'When you read these lines I shall be dead.'

'Dead?' I said. 'Dead?'

(I spoke out loud and clear. Mario stopped crying and stared at me.)

'She's dead,' Mario said.

'How did she die?' I said. I ran over to him and grasped him by the shoulders. 'Tell me how she died and why you left her there alone. You can't die just like that—your heart doesn't stop beating for nothing. Mine hasn't stopped, neither has yours. There must have been something that stopped it. What was it?—tell me. I don't know, but there was something, there was something.'

I looked round the room, petrified: what desolation, what misery there was in me. The world was crashing down on me, the houses were burying me. And yet, lying in a heap like that with Mario's body under me, some mysterious force brought me back to reality. I needed someone to soothe away my pain, and an urge sprang up in me like the old times when we made love together, when his hands ran or lingered over my skin and made it prickle with joy.

I looked at his hands—oh, I loved those man's hands for my poor woman's skin!

And then I pressed down heavier on him, and he let me do it. I tried to take off his raincoat, and it was when I was scrabbling to get his arms out of the sleeves that he suddenly turned round. I had never seen his eyes look like they did then.

They seemed to be shot through with blood.

'Keep still, you whore!' he shouted. 'Keep still!'

He was clenching and unclenching his hands. Then he held them open in front of my face.

'You see,' he shouted, 'you see—I strangled her with these.'

XXX

The police came and searched everything. There were big headlines in the papers, and in one or two there were pictures of Anna. They told a whole lot of lies and invented details; they wrote about me too, and said lots of nasty things.

I didn't see Mario again. That night it was raining he went and told the police everything; he ran out of my room, and the din woke up the people in the *pensione* and they all came to see what was going on because Mario was shouting.

The police questioned me and I told them all I knew about Anna; I said I was fond of her, and she'd been fond of me. They showed me her corpse: the police made me look at her. Anna was still the same, with her lovely face; her eyes were wide open. I kissed Anna, I put my arms round her, but Anna didn't wake, she didn't speak another word to me.

The police took Anna's exercise book and read

everything she had written. They were rough men who used bad language; they threw Anna's clothes all over the place, and mine too.

I asked them to let me read Anna's exercise book, because I'd read only the first few words. The police finally handed it over because they said I might be able to explain some obscure points. But there weren't any obscure points. It was all very clear.

Anna was dead because she had to die; for a long time she had wanted to die—even that first day I met her she had talked of dying. I told all this to the police, but they laughed; they said that a man had been responsible for her death and he would be punished.

I knew very well that Mario had done it only because Anna wasn't capable herself; Anna had used him, she had led him on to do it. Mario wasn't guilty. Anna wasn't guilty. Nobody was guilty. In any case Anna had explained it all.

'One afternoon', she had written, 'I went out for a walk. I walked about, as I always do, but I was uneasy. The sun was shining, and there were so many people out in the streets.

'Suddenly I got weighed down with that old feeling of melancholy: it made every step difficult, every movement painful. I got on a tram—one that went out to the Ponte Milvio.

'It was an old tram, all rickety and shaky; the seats ran longways—two wooden benches opposite each other. I sat down among those people with their bags and parcels . . . a lot of them must have been going out into the country for a picnic.

'I don't know why, but my eyes got fixed on all those feet lined up in front of me, all those shoes.

'There were so many of them.

'Feet and shoes—women's, men's, old men's, old women's—and just two belonging to a child, which were hanging down in mid-air. All the shoes were worn out, ugly, dusty, even those with some pretensions to smartness, the ones with buckles and laces.

'The child had on brown leather shoes with pointed toes; they were too small for him and his big toes stuck out in their light brown socks.

'I wasn't thinking of anything, I was just looking.

'The tram went clanking over the bridge and ran along to the terminus; I got off and went and sat on a patch of grass by the Tiber. I looked at the water, I stared dully at it. I fixed my eyes on a point in midstream: the water kept moving, moving. Sometimes rubbish came floating down —a twig, some dead leaves, a piece of paper; if the rubbish dropped out of the current it came to a standstill near my patch of grass where the water was still and seemed stagnant. I liked that part of the Tiber—it was a nice river.

'I stayed down there a long time. I wanted to feel if the water was cold. You told me that once, in the summer, you bathed there. But I couldn't summon up the courage; I reckoned it would be child's play to slip down the bank, and yet I was too scared.

'So I went back into the city, but I didn't catch a tram, I went in on foot—I walked all the way along the Via Flaminia which was crowded with people . . . it must have been a Sunday.

'The Via Flaminia never seemed to finish—what an endless street, and what a lot of noise!

'When I was back in the centre I made my way for no particular reason to Mario's place.

'You'll say now I shouldn't have gone there; Mario was nothing to me, and I was nothing to him. But I had met him that time when we both went to see him, and then that time when he came to see us, and I knew a lot about him . . . you had told me lots of things—that way he had of laughing, the cruel way he used to knock you about, and how you used to love each other in such an animal way.

'You see, I'm writing all this as if I were already dead.

'I have the feeling my words are weak and lifeless. That's because I died that afternoon, not long ago. Nobody killed me—there was just that deep melancholy in me.

'My body dried up that afternoon.

'I realised it as I was going back along the Via Flaminia, walking among all those people; I had got on the wrong pavement, I was going against the stream and people were pushing and jostling me; I should have moved over to the right, I know, and instead I went left, I had no idea which was the right way to go.

'They were all pushing me, but I didn't feel a thing. At times I would suddenly picture the river again, and sometimes that child's shoes with pointed toes.

'Then I went up the stairs to Mario's place, and went into the room that had once been yours. He was lying there on the bed with his coat over him, just like the first time.

' "*Ciao*, Anna," he said. He seemed to be in a good mood.

'I remembered that little caress he gave me that night, that time in the dark when he touched my face, and his cold hand rested on my face, and you didn't say anything, you let him caress you too.

' "*Ciao*," I said, "I've come to see you."

'I liked calling him *tu*, and Mario liked it too. I lay down next to him because I was cold. I've told you already that inside I was all dried up and empty—the sun that afternoon had passed over my skin without warming it.

'He started talking about you, and he asked where you were. I said I didn't know. Perhaps you'd stayed at home, I said.

'And I said you didn't know I had come to see him, and I didn't want you to know. This pleased him—he was a man, after all, and he immediately thought, from my dubious behaviour, that he was on to a good thing. But I only told him that because I didn't want to hurt you, I didn't want you to get the wrong idea.

'That day I didn't stay long with him, I soon came away; I had done nothing you could criticise me for, and yet when I saw you at home, and saw you had made supper, I felt guilty because I was hiding something from you. You were so quiet and sweet that day. You didn't suspect a thing.

'It's difficult to explain it all, it's difficult to analyse what was going on in my mind just then.

'After that first time I went again to Mario's.

'He was dead keen to see me, he didn't hide it, but I knew very well he didn't love me, any more than I loved him. He was playing a game with me . . . but he didn't know that I was playing, too.

'Sure, we kissed—sure, my body responded to his, or rather he thought it responded. In fact my body was cold and was only submitting; my mouth was frozen even though Mario warmed it. In my mind I was always miles away; I was wandering in my lovely meadows full of flowers, I didn't want anything more to do with the world; the men on this earth were a small thing, and I wanted to reach out to a world where there were no children's pointed shoes, no crowded places with people pushing me, and shameful instincts to be satisfied.

'I was taking revenge on myself, I was being an animal for the last time. I was touching the bottom . . . but surely, I thought, I shall come up again.'

XXXI

'I don't know if you ever got to know Mario as I've done these last few weeks.

'I spent many hours with him, and sometimes I didn't come home; when I came back late the following morning I used to see the reproachful look in your eyes, but I kept on doing it—I had to keep on.

'Mario's like lots of others; this horrible society of ours produces so many of his type. When they were small children they played and laughed and went to school; then they grew up and everything in them changed. I'm a bit like that too. Many times, when Mario and I talked together, we tried to explain why we were reduced to this (he didn't know what to say, he always said, "I've reached rock bottom"). But if you only knew how maddening and impossible it was to fathom out. When I look back on some of the things that have happened in the last few years, the people we live among, this place we call *home* ("I was born here," they say, "this is my home"), everything seems a wreck . . . the eternal values are gone— purity, goodness, love for our fellow creatures. I, you, Mario and all the others we know—we're lost and all alone in a marvellous world where there's still a sky, where the sun rises and sets, but deep down in us there's nothing left, we wear out our nails, scraping and digging to see if something will come out.

'I used to say to Mario, "What are you doing in this room? Go out, get cracking."

'(I used to say that, not because I wanted to get cracking as well and go out with him, and forget, and make a new start—it was different for me—but only because I hoped that he, being a man, would pull himself together, think things out, have a definite aim, and perhaps go back to you.)

'But it's just as useless with him as with all the others. Mario's shut up in himself, and so are you. You and I spent a lot of time together, but I realise we didn't find a way out.

'So all that was left for me was my body, and I used it to get him excited. Mario was nauseated, and so was I; he hated me—he used me as a way of paying himself back for all the time he'd lost, when you left him. You were so submissive, you let him use you. And I humiliated myself too, by letting him use me, but deep down in my heart I used to pray it would all be over soon.

'It would have been a sweet death for me, and I'd been looking forward to it for so long. You know I'm too much of a coward ever to have managed it myself—I needed somebody to do it for me. That somebody I knew could be Mario.

'I knew it could be him, when he squeezed me so roughly and arrogantly; those arms of his were hard, the muscles were firm. It was an embrace without love, with no pleasure in it—he seemed to want to annihilate me, destroy me.

'We were enemies: when Mario laughed in that hysterical way that you know, after throwing himself on top of me or down at my side, I sensed he could kill me, and the certainty of it made me shudder. It wouldn't have taken anything to spark him off.

'Perhaps Mario needs to kill somebody. He's had a lot of deaths in his family; one day he told me he's got nobody left in the world—just that money of his he doesn't know what to do with. He said that corpses get filled with worms, that the body falls to pieces, that all the flesh rots away. Often I noticed he suddenly stopped talking and stared in front of him; then he would push me and shove me out.

'He's selfish, we're all selfish.

'I'm waiting for the moment when he'll make up his mind. He doesn't know I can drive him into doing what I want.

'Now, if he laughs, I laugh too; we laugh in a mournful way in that room in the Piazza di

Pietra. I've noticed the room is rather isolated from the rest of the house: even if I shout nobody's going to hear—it would be terrible if somebody came in and saved me.

'I don't know what method Mario will use to kill me, but sometimes when his heavy hands nearly break me in two I dream of those hands round my neck.

'I hear my breath gurgling in my throat, and a cry comes out . . . it must be horrible and yet marvellous to look with open eyes down into the abyss where my spirit will fall.

'You see, it doesn't take much to die—I realise that now. It only needs brute force, just the pressure of two fingers with strong bones. Then I shall twist and writhe like a shrub in a blazing fire.'

XXXII

'Forgive me if I write this for you.

'I found this poor old exercise book among my papers not long ago; it was new once—I remember when I bought it, I used it for exercises at school, and then it got left in a drawer for years, and I forgot all about it. Now I'm writing these last words in it. As I write I look up and I see you in the corner watching me.

'Let me go on writing, dear, don't interrupt me.

'I know that winter's over, it's not cold any more, we can even leave the window open; but these seasons that come and go—spring, summer, then autumn, winter, the year that changes name, and the months—it's just time and it means nothing to me any more. You tell me—what's the point in waiting for these seasons to come round?

'Once, in my "manuscript", I wrote about the disgusting urges in my body, about the way I got caught up in a false horrible love . . . but the manuscript takes me back in time—it's all an old story now. I spoke of the two Annas—Anna and the other one; the real Anna has been dead for heaven knows how long, and the other one has nothing to go on living for because something has died in her, her disgusting organs which brought her that empty joy are all worn out.

'They no longer throb with life.

'I've realised that during these last few days. Mario doesn't do anything for me.

'Yesterday I went walking for the last time through the lovely streets of Rome.

'I didn't go yesterday to Mario's place; I said goodbye to the city.

'Then I went and sat on the steps round the obelisk in the Piazza del Popolo. The lions were spouting water, children were climbing up and sitting on them. I helped one child climb up. He was a little boy with blue eyes, like the one Anna dreamed of some nights when she wanted to be happy.

' "What's your name?" I asked.

' "Paolo," the little boy replied.

' "Paolo," I said. "I used to know another boy with that name."

' "Who was that?" the little boy said.

' "Another Paolo."

' "One of my friends is called Paolo, the same as me," said the little boy, "so perhaps that's who you mean."

' "No, it's not that one. Mine's dead."

'The little boy was silent and looked at me as he sat astride the stone lion. He had a sad expression. "What's your name?" he said.

' "Anna."

' "I know a girl who's called Anna. We often play together."

' "What games do you play?"

' "We play running," the little boy said. "But I can't catch Anna—she runs too fast."

' "So does she catch you?" I asked.

'The little boy blushed and said the little girl always caught him.

'I stayed there a long time with that little boy until the Piazza turned violet and the trees caught fire with the setting sun. Then his mother came to take him home. The little boy waved goodbye.'

XXXIII

Here Anna's exercise book came to an end. I had to give it back to the police—they said they needed it for their enquiries. What enquiries they had to make, I don't know—after all, it had all happened, there was no going back.

I also had to see Mario: they put us facing each other, and listened carefully to what we said. But we didn't say much; I felt like crying, but I made a great effort to stop myself—I didn't want to show any weakness in front of those people.

They were outsiders, trying to find out about us—horrible people who thought they had the right to pry into what we had done. When Anna, and I, and Mario, and all the others were hitting our heads against the wall, nobody took any notice of us, nobody could put us right, nothing— if we'd been corpses lying stiff in the gutter, they'd only have kicked us. But now it was different, now they wanted to know all about us, they were planning how to punish us.

Society came in when it was all over and wanted to say its piece.

I looked at the faces of those people—not only the police, and the magistrates, but the others, the people in the *pensione,* and also Antonio who had come creeping back on the scene, and the people in the city who knew me—they all looked at me in an odd way, and wanted to give me advice. Before that, they'd all gone their own way. Now we couldn't move for them.

But I was conscious only of pain, a thorn planted in my flesh: Anna was dead—Anna, that gentle dark creature.

Sometimes I used to say, 'What are you doing, Anna—where are you now?'

I imagined her meeting Paolo, the only man she loved as a young girl: they would go off alone, and forget about human things.

I was still living in Anna's room; the plants on the roof garden were turning green and coming into flower. Sometimes Antonio would knock on the door and come in, and we would talk about her. He was clumsy and didn't know anything, yet his mouth tasted fresh. He showed me a photograph of the girl from Terni; perhaps he would marry her one day. He talked calmly about the girl, and calmly let me kiss him.

I could hear Anna's voice saying, 'He's a little lamb.'

He had fairish hair and a pink complexion. He was strongly built, and his muscles swelled under his jacket. He had a quiet smiling expression.

When I looked at him I was angry; I thought of hurricanes and I wanted raging elements to wipe out cities and people, I wanted the earth to howl its contempt at the cold distant sky, and I wanted creatures to be united by love. But the most terrible thing was being left alone. Anna was dead, and I had nobody else.

There was Antonio—he was still there, and there were millions of other beings still there . . . I would come across them everywhere, at all times. That was the desperate thing.

So I kissed him; and when I did it I felt as if the world was suffocating me. Up from my feet, right through my body and into my blood came the quiet wisdom of those who never think, who don't demand to know beyond a certain limit.

Sometimes, when I thought of Anna, a terribly sharp pain cut through me, but it was envy, a pang of fear that I wouldn't reach the peace of those solitary places where there are no seasons, no years succeeding years. All I was left with was earthly days—getting up, going out, walking— mean trivial things.

All I was left with was the evening that keeps coming round, the night that howls with cold, the morning that shivers. The story of Anna had come full circle and was closed: I was left trapped inside.